Intimidator

Book Two

PREYFINDERS

Cari Silverwood

Copyright 2014 Cari Silverwood
Published by Cari Silverwood
Editor: Nerine Dorman
Cover Artist: Thomas Dorman aka Dr. Benway on Deviantart and Facebook
Formatter: Polgarus Studio

All rights reserved. This copy is intended for the original purchaser of this e-book only. No part of this e-book may be reproduced, scanned, or distributed in any printed or electronic form without prior written permission from the author. Please do not participate in or encourage piracy of copyrighted materials.

This e-book is a work of fiction. While reference might be made to actual historical events or existing locations, the names, characters, places and incidents are either the product of the author's imagination or are used fictitiously, and any resemblance to actual persons, living or dead, business establishments, events, or locales is entirely coincidental.

Acknowledgement

To Jennifer Zeffer, my latest cheerleader and reader, for dealing with my addiction to praise while I write.

I also need to thank my wonderful beta readers Bianca Sarble and Khloe Wren (both are fellow Australian erotic authors), and Leia Shaw, writer of erotic, paranormal, and New Adult fiction.

About Intimidator

Willow has her hands full scraping out a life in a grungy neighborhood where drugs and crime are the norm. Life is hard, but it's about to get harder. Being transformed into a sexual pet for an alien warrior may be her only way out.

But Stom, the man she's been awarded to as a battle honor, has no use for a female, not when his heart is still in a million pieces.

Though the need to be Stom's mate is overwhelming her, mending his heart isn't going to be enough. His enemies are searching, looking for the women who are more than they seem, and she's in their hands before she discovers she's more-than-human.

Sometimes it sucks to be a chosen one.

Book One, Precious Sacrifice is in the erotic anthology, Kept, but will soon be released as a solo book.

The books of Preyfinders are joined like links on a chain. Here is the last small piece of Precious Sacrifice and the first piece of Intimidator.

Epilogue from Book 1, Precious Sacrifice

Talia Wolfe squatted among the dust and a few bird droppings. The pigeons had made their home here already. After her sob-story and a small bribe, one of the rescue crew had let her in. She used the katana to scratch an arc in the rubble. The huge gap in the wall and the missing balcony made this seem unfamiliar, as if it wasn't even Brittany's place.

Slowly she rose, feeling the skintight black jeans grip her tightly. She squirmed a little as pleasant sensations throbbed outward. Ugh. There was an odd vibe in the air here, almost sexual. It clashed horribly with the sadness.

Talia shook her head, tilted her neck back to strive to stop the flow of tears, but they ran down her face anyway. She coughed and swallowed, wiped her eyes with her sleeve.

Stop crying. Crying wasn't helping.

She might be a lab person and not a field investigator, but she wasn't giving up on finding out what had really happened here. Her baby sister was missing and no way was she ever presuming her dead.

"I'll find out what happened to you, Brit, if I have to tear this whole fucking building apart to find clues."

She stepped up to the hole and looked down at the organized chaos below. Sirens whooped and wailed in the distance. People in orange jackets worked with cranes and trucks to shift rubble and save people. This had been an earthquake?

She stuck the sword into the floor and leaned on it a little, refreshed by the gusts flailing at the building and cooling her face. Absolute sacrilege to use a sword so, but who was going to chastise her?

"I'm finding you, sis. I am."

A scrabbling made her swivel to the side. A man crouched there, drool dripping from his mouth. He'd somehow scrambled up from below. That whole corner of the apartment was gone.

He coughed and spat blood, swayed. A pistol swung in one lowered hand. That alone made her wary, let alone the drool and spaced-out look. She unwedged the sword from the floor, raised it a tad.

No need to panic. Even if he's got a pistol, and I've got a bloody sword. Ever since she was a teen she'd had a knack with pointy things, and could make them do stuff no one else could.

With the rioting and unrest below, she figured she had a right to be straightforward, especially when he took a staggery step toward her and his arm began to swing up.

"Don't do anything, mister. I don't know you." The hoarse tone must have impressed him. He paused and looked back with narrowing eyes. If only her students were as well behaved. "Good. You keep yours down and I'll keep mine. I suggest you leave now –"

He chuckled low and from the twitch of his wrist he was going to raise that gun and aim at her.

Fuck. Her bluff was called.

Practicing kendo and her innate talent meant she could theoretically kill. If you forgot he was a person. Too far to reach with a swing. She'd have to throw. A knife, yes, but a sword – a full sword? Something, a weird *zing* in the air here, grabbed her, made her think she could do this.

She swept up the sword, leaning and twisting to the side to gain momentum for the throw.

Then someone dropped from the hole in the roof, landing between her and droolman, dark coat swirling like a fucking superhero. She swore. The floor shuddered at the sudden weight. Something cracked even. Was he that heavy? Or the floor that weak?

A flurry of blows and she stepped to the side, watching their little fight, hearing the grunts. The new guy was big and mean, and didn't hold back his strikes at all. Neither did drooly man. The pistol went flying, so did a small sword… What the fuck? Who else but her used a sword? Then drooly man poised another knife above the guy ready to drive it into the juncture of neck and shoulder. Instant death zone.

No. She really didn't want him, her would-be rescuer, to die.

She gulped, and threw. Knew it was a thousand to one. A trillion to one. Impossible. Wasn't a straight throw. Men were in the way, like the big guy. She had to go and bounce it off things like the wall to the left. It was a fucking hard ricochet, an incredibly stupid throw. The blade whipped round, hit wall, spun, bounced and flew.

Impossible, incredible, *doable.*

The blade sank, all two feet of shiny, pointy metal, into drool man's side. Heart level. He gasped once and froze at the same time as there was a *whoompfh,* and much of him turned into particle-sized bits of flesh. The cloud of red splattered across what was left of the corner of the room.

Big guy let the remains of his opponent slide to the floor and he turned to her, empty hand emerging from his coat. His mint green eyes glinted.

"What the fuck was that?" She frowned. He'd shot the guy with something, hadn't he?

Damn. What was *he*? His face looked like someone had used him for carving practice then painted it blue. As he came toward her, she stepped back, wishing her sword wasn't currently residing in a mangled corpse. Her heel hit something hard and she stopped. "Who are you?"

"Brask. Who are you?"

She guessed it was okay to answer. "Talia Wolfe, I'm looking for my sister, Brittany. Though seeing you just killed someone that might take priority."

"She's not here."

"Obviously. I'm glad I saved you."

He grunted.

Ungrateful imbecile. She felt in the pocket of her jacket, hoping to find a weapon, and only came up with some origami paper. Sometimes, in deep dreams, she imagined herself with a sword of paper that cut *anything*. Boy, could she use one of them now.

Brask was wide enough to blot out the sun. And that blue war paint made him seem worse. Not that his semi-spiky blond hairdo wasn't scary too. Where did he get his make-up and hair styling done?

"Who was that?" She twitched her head at the dead man, and managed to keep down breakfast. Jeez. She could clamp down on her emotions, but he was a mess and enough to upset anyone not tranquilized.

"A Bak-lal clone." At her frown Brask gave her a mirthless smile. "Recon observed him climb up out of the collapsed building next to us. He was a killer, made by an alien. He should be the last one."

Was he crazy? "That's some wild story." Or was it that wild? Things, here, now, felt so odd. Like anything could happen.

He shrugged and made as if to come closer.

"Stop right there." She held out her palm.

And he grabbed it, twisted her wrist, stepped in fast, and clasped her neck in his other hand.

He glared. Green eyes. Big green eyes. A flash shocked her to her very bones, tinkling through her like broken glass. As she crumpled, she was distantly aware of him catching her, along with a ringing in her ears that swept her body. Goose bumps rose and her hair stood on end.

"Sleep," he whispered. "Forget, pretty girl." His hand brushed her cheek, scraping her skin yet gentle. "I'm sorry I had to do this. I wish…"

Wish what?

She rallied, blinking and frowning at the blurred face. "What?"

"Still with me? Huh."

The flash came again.

Bastard. She felt her eyes roll up. Her hand encountered someone's hard-muscled shoulder and slid. Through the fog in her mind, his delicious male scent registered. She opened her eyes again.

"What are you? I need to do this three times?"

Flash.

Words drifted by. "I swear, if you were on the death list, and I was allowed on a Hunt –" The voice dulled then faded back in. "– and make you my pet."

A strange rapture possessed her, where she became him and he melted into her. And then, she *forgot…*

*****

On the other side of the continent of Australia, something long buried stirred, and listened to the signals from its killed sister queen. Now, it decided, would be a good time to fire up the stagnant engines and set out a plan of conquest.

Chapter 1

On the planet Grearth.

The wind came from where the sun bleached the horizon, fluttering the ashes higher off the scorched ground, a bitter flock of blackness that clouded the sky for miles. Stom sucked in a breath through his mask. Unlike the trail of ten fighting men who swept out to his left and right, he'd removed his helmet – the goggles and the mask with a breathing filter was it. He needed the touch of the breeze on his face, no matter how acrid.

On his retinal map, there was a tiny green triangle at this spot. This had once been his home.

Nasskia, little Bon, and her older brother Septis would lie here, somewhere, buried underneath the ash at his feet. Unless they'd been unlucky and the Bak-lal had taken them, changed them; if so, they could be anywhere on Grearth. Their nerves hard-wired. Their skin armored, their brains pumped with instructions from the nearest factory queen. Their personalities gone. Even the little ones like Bon. His throat tightened, his eyes stung, and a small muscle beside his eye twitched.

Despite the tight-held ball of emotions inside him, Stom treated his environs to another careful visual sweep. Nothing moved.

Elger's voice buzzed in his ear comm. "It's clear, Stom. We haven't seen a Bak soldier for days."

With their leader dead three days ago, Stom was filling in. He grunted affirmation to Elger. Other patrols had been ambushed; theirs had been relatively lucky for three days running. "Rest. Keep your eyes up."

He hunched down onto his heels but kept his mech rifle in his hands. The last Baks on this part of the continent had been a weedy, damaged force. Maybe they could cleanse the whole planet. Never been done before, but gods, they needed to.

There'd never been a starfarer home planet invaded before. How the Bak-lal had achieved this was a mystery. In one night, the Bak-lal had appeared in armies of converted people and insect beast machines.

Once, above his head would've swayed a tangled canopy of trees. Grearth, forest planet.

He felt his hand move on the padding inside his glove. His skin was striped with black, his color the mark of the Feya, a people born under trees.

When it had happened, he'd been off planet. A few million had been evacuated. Some higher up had held off using the Planet Breakers and instead ordered Grearth razed by flame. The difference had seemed miniscule. Turn the planet into dust, or burn it. He'd watched from holoscreen as they'd detonated the bombs, the firestorms rendered in deep reds, oranges and black. The superheated carpet of fire had crept silently across the world, burning everything to nothing.

Yet the evidence before his eyes had meant zero. He hadn't believed, not until they'd been dropped in to clean up remnants.

At least someone would have a future here, maybe not for a hundred years, but the world would recover. He stared bleakly outward, vision blurred. Nasskia was gone. His bond mate. His heart. His soul. His one and only Nasskia who could never be replaced, and his little ones. May demons take the Bak-lal; his little ones were gone too.

His eyes stung with wetness again, but he refused to blink, sniff or show weakness. Someone would make this land green and well again, just not him.

Slowly he stood, with a handful of his burnt land in his left fist. He opened his hand, and let it fall away. The acrid smell penetrated his mask.

Before him, on the ground, among the fragments of burned earth and wood and perhaps Feya, the black grit stirred. An eye blinked up at him.

A creature surged upright in an eruption of black, its arms reaching for him. The ashes whirled. To either side, other scorched figures flew up, uncovering themselves and lunging at his armored warriors. Without hesitation, he shot the one in front of him, then swung his rifle and shot those fighting his men when he could. Pieces of Bak-lal soldier splattered and joined the dark floating flecks. At least none of these had grown weapons from their limbs. Those ones were difficult to kill.

As always when they met the converted, he repeated the words in his head. *Not people. Not people, not anymore.*

Screams began.

His men were dying.

A new thing. Some of the enemy planted glowing hands on his men.

"My armor's melting!" While the soldier staggered back, a second Bak speared the soldier's chest and slaughtered him.

Stom shot that one too. The crack and whiplash whistles of homing rounds drummed in his ears. The jerk of the rifle jarred his arm, as he fired and fired and thumped the stock into the Baks that rushed in close.

By the end he was panting, sweating, his rifle empty, his armor scarred by yellow goo that still bubbled and hissed. The last Bak-lal he'd shot lay before him, nerves dangling from its shattered neck in loops of glinting wire. A small one, this. Tiny.

He swallowed then turned and walked away.

Elger flicked his gaze across the body and said the obvious. "A child."

"Yes." Then he whispered more words to himself, as if he could make them true by pure force of will. "Not mine. Not. Mine. No. Kak, no." Choking, he splayed his gloved hand over his face. "Please, god, no."

The barrel of his abused rifle steamed, smoke curling from the end. For a second he swayed, dizzy.

His comm came alive. The Baks were rising again all over the planet. They'd been buried and factory queens were somewhere deep under the ground, waiting, replenishing from stored bodies, remaking their soldiers deadlier than before.

That was the last day his planet existed. He became an orphan. Adrift.

He left with the survivors. They brought in the Planet Breakers. The command ship showed the destruction of Grearth on screen for anyone who wanted to see the planet break apart, but he hadn't watched. Instead, he'd been in his bunk room cleaning weapons and armor. If he couldn't be the giver of life, he would be the bringer of death.

For many battles, he threw himself into the very worst of the fighting. He didn't pray for his death because he wanted to live so that he could kill more of *them*. But the day came when he did too much and they awarded him some paltry thing, and they took him away from his game with death. Diplomacy said he must accept the accolades. And so he smiled and shook hands and said yes.

When the ship carrying him emerged from warp space, he beheld the blue-and-green planet Earth.

"This will not take long." Once they matched him up, he'd find this pet, like they wanted him to, lose her, leave. What did he want with females? An honorable Feya male took one and only one partner in his lifetime.

He'd play this game, and accept this battle honor, only as far as he had to so as not to insult anyone.

Nasskia. His Nasskia. He wept for the first time.

*****

With the woman leaning on her, Willow had to struggle to get the keys out of her handbag. Whatever drug Kasper had given her wasn't wearing off. Not surprising really. Poor thing. As long as she didn't get worse…

She kept her arm around the girl's waist and kept rummaging. One day someone would make keys that wormed through all the other crap in your handbag and leaped into your hand. Then she'd probably die of a heart attack.

Using her arm, Willow nudged the opening of the bag wider. She peered in. If she could see past her nose it would be a bonus too.

She really should get the porch light fixed.

"Where the hell are you?" she muttered. "Ah!"

The girl made small moaning noises as she inserted the key in the lock and jiggled it, searching for the angle that would engage the frickin' stupid damn lock.

Kasper would have found out someone had stolen his victim by now. She'd seen him touch the girl's drink. He'd spiked it. Must have. While he was talking to someone, the woman had slowly slumped into the corner at her seat near the ladies' restroom. She'd heard through the gossip at the pub that Kasper had done this before. Dope 'em, get them back to his house, rape them, party on, let the boys do them again, then let them go miles away.

No one around here seemed game to tell the cops when they came investigating. Or if they had, there'd been no evidence found.

Lucky for this girl... *Was her name Monique?* Luckily, it'd been the end of her shift. After three rum and cokes, nobody was this knocked out, and it was definitely three. She'd served two of them herself.

Breathe slowly.

"Hey, girl, Monique? Is that you? Maybe you can tell me a number I can call?"

Just as she found the spot for the key, a car pulled up behind them, headlights blazing across the neighborhood. Loud music cut off and a door slammed.

She swallowed, feeling the scrape as the key rotated against metal. Once inside, she'd be safe. The house repelled angry people like it was anti-matter for angry. Crazy but true. Boyfriends with their knickers in a twist never made it through the door. If they got angry while inside, they never stayed long. It had to work on Kasper too, didn't it?

This old house of her aunt's was Castle Freaky. It wasn't normal but she'd given up trying to figure out how or why, years ago, soon after her aunt died.

The key turned all the way. *Click.* The door swung open.

"Hey. Where the fuck are you going?" The low, menacing voice carried yards in the night air. She'd heard Kasper talk like that to a man lying gasping on the ground, two seconds before he kicked him in the guts. "That's my girl you've got there. Did you ask her if she wants to go in?"

From the sounds, they'd leaped over the gate and there were too many footsteps to be from only one man.

Go, go, go. She did *not* want Kasper as her enemy but she ignored him. She staggered in with the girl weighing down her shoulder, then swiveled and kicked the door shut. It locked automatically. Someone jumped onto the porch, and there was silence, except for the harsh male breathing inches away, on the other side of the door.

He spoke again. "You better never, ever, turn your back on me again."

Cold tendrils crackled into her flesh.

Shit. Her eyes refused to close. He was going to punch his fist through the timber any second. Still holding the keys tight so they wouldn't jingle, she gave him the finger.

Asshole.

"Get out here!" A kick slammed into the door and shook a boom through the house.

Her hand trembled. She swept back a twirl of hair dangling across her eye.

She did nothing more – didn't move, didn't talk, tried not to breathe.

A minute passed. Another. Something made long dragging scratches on the other side of the door. *Scre-e-eetch. Scritch.* Her heart cowered down small and painful in her chest. It might stop beating, she was that scared. It hadn't taken this long with that craziest boyfriend, Alan, had it?

She heard the thumps of footsteps on the porch again then car doors opened and shut. Maybe they were pretending? *Maybe, maybe, maybe* ran frantic circles in her mind, bouncing off the walls, while she waited for some new frightening sound.

The engine revved and they drove away, the noise lessening, dwindling, gone.

Fuck. Light-headed from breathing barely enough for a mouse, she opened her mouth and hauled in a long draught of air.

Muscles braced, she let the girl slide slowly to the floor where she lay in a pile.

"God." She took another big shuddery lungful. "God dammit. Don't you throw up on our rug."

She hadn't wanted Kasper to know. Phoning for an ambulance or maybe driving the girl to the hospital ER had been her first plan. But after she bundled Monique into her car, the girl had started crying about not wanting the cops involved. When Kasper exited the pub a few yards in front of her car, she'd made a snap decision – take her home. After all, she lived only three streets from the pub and Monique seemed okay, just plastered.

He knew though, he did. Disaster.

Bright side, he hadn't punched in the flimsy door or broken a window to come in that way. The freaky house effect had worked.

She grinned. Kasper was the big bad wolf trying to blow the house down.

Problem was, she had to leave sometime. What *had* she been thinking?

The lights were on down the hallway. The girl lay curled on the floor, breathing quietly and drooling on the rug. Her blond hair was as short as Willow's black curls. She looked sweet and terribly innocent even if her skirt was petite enough to show glimpses of her panties, her upper arm had a bleeding heart tattoo…and she was in trouble with the cops.

What was she going to do with her? "Monique! You got some angry guys after us. Can I call the cops now? Monique?"

The croaked *no* and the head shake that stirred the rug were determined.

"What the hell did you do? Rob a bank? A church? Flick a booger on a cop?" She stuck her splayed fingers in her hair. "What am I going to do with you now? Maybe I can have you stuffed and mounted on my mantelpiece?" Pity she had no mantelpiece. She yelled out, "Ally? You there?"

She hadn't thought at all. Now she'd gone and involved Ally, her younger cousin, the one she'd protected all these years, and for what? To get them both killed by some dickhead when they went to get groceries?

"I'm here." Ally trudged out of her bedroom and stood blinking at her, in her PJs, clutching her teddy bear. Twenty-three, she still had a teddy, and Ally was as scatterbrained and out of this world as they came. "Who's that, Will?" She frowned down at their guest.

Maybe Ally could help? Though if her meds for the night had kicked in, she might be too drowsy to think straight. That she'd taken this long to emerge after all that ruckus, and wasn't spazzing out like a frightened Bambi, meant she must have swallowed them a while ago.

"Monique. I think that's her name… You're always on the 'net. Seen her in any crime stories?"

"Not that I remember." Ally knelt and tucked the bear into the girl's hand.

The girl looked up at them blearily. "Will? You're a boy?"

She grunted. It wasn't worth explaining the whole Will was short for Willow thing.

Actually, Ally was so agoraphobic she barely left the house. The only one likely to get grabbed or assaulted by Kasper was her. And the house *had* worked its magic. In the past, boyfriends had totally forgotten arguments. As in gone, completely. Willow sucked on her lip. If Kasper forgot, truly, she could use this.

She'd play it cool for a few days and listen to see if people heard about her Good Samaritan blooper. She thought about the neighborhood with the heroin and crack addicts, the gangs, the occasional stupid violence. On the days that she walked in to work, she had to take care not to step on needles. If anything like this happened again, no way was she standing aside to let someone be abused.

She'd tread carefully for a while. Willow leaned back against the door and patted the panel. *Good house.*

She could use this if she had the balls. Fuck sitting around and watching shit happen. Who else ever got the chance to be the superhero?

You can only die once.

Willow frowned. Bad saying. *When life serves you lemons, make lemonade? When the shit hits the fan, get a shovel?*

Yeah, one of those. Definitely not the dying one.

When she went outside in the morning and found *SLUT HOWSE* written in blood on the door, she didn't change her mind. Who listened to bad spellers anyway?

But she scrubbed it off before Ally could see it.

*****

The Bak-lal factory queen examined the altered human through the eyes of the little spidery rover. The metal legs snicked quietly as they extracted his breathing tube. The human gasped and coughed up blood and phlegm then stared unfocused for a few seconds before sitting up on the table. More blood specked the places on his hands and feet where she'd first pierced him.

"Are you aware and functioning correctly, Christopher One?" The rover's voice came out with an over-riding buzz but then nothing was perfect after so many years.

At least human technology had advanced enough to allow use of some of their machinery. The many legs of Raska's true body twitched where they were tucked, hundreds of yards deep into the surrounding soil. Exciting, this was.

One day soon, she might burrow upwards, emerge, and stride across the surface.

"I am. Functioning. Correctly." The man blinked slower than a normal human but it was sufficient to moisturize his eyes. The brain had suffered during transformation.

For a micro-second, the factory queen, Raska, ran through the statistics and the predicted arcs of the events she planned. Nothing was certain. She had poor brain function for a queen and knew it. The fight damage from the ancient battle was irreparable.

Because of that, interstellar communication was impossible from the surface, let alone buried as she was. Her sister factory queen had been destroyed due to poor calculation of risk. She would be careful and slow and sure.

Soon, though, *soon, soon, soon,* she would call, she would succeed, and the rest of her family would arrive from space in a vast fleet of Bak-lal.

Until then, one human convert at a time. No multiple clones, not this time. That had somehow triggered an alert in the Preyfinder's database. A small yet effective army was best.

This room inside her body was small compared to the others with assembly lines that stood idle, waiting to spit out soldiers. Frustrating, to have to be so simple. *Wait,* she whispered to herself. *Wait. I am crippled.*

"Can you return to your home now, Christopher One?"

"Yes." He nodded.

"How?" The question would be a final test of the creature's reasoning. Fail and he would be terminated like several before him.

"I will fly. I will go to the airport." He shook his head and his speech became smoother. "I've still got the ticket I came here on. Return trip. Brisbane to Adelaide and back again."

This one, Christopher, would be the first to go back, a vanguard in another city, the city where her factory queen sister had reigned until she died. Because there, somehow, the data Raska tasted insisted there were anomalies – there were human females whose parameters existed outside the norm.

She had gathered data from everywhere since her sister's death, even tasted remnants of the brain of Jonathan Two that had been unearthed from the rubble by a brave rover. The rover had limped to her with that fragment of preserved brain.

The taste had been electric. The pieces had slotted in. A female bond-mated to an Igrakk warrior. A woman with a sparrow *familiar*. The fact had led to an avalanche of strange information.

Witches. Myths. Lies?

Fact: An eruption of healing that had temporarily healed even the Jonathan clone. Exceptional data. Extraordinary. Paranormal, said the human sources she'd searched. Best of all, there were tantalizing hints and tastes of more, back there, in Brisbane, her sister's city.

More, more, more.

If these witches existed, she would find them, take them for her own.

"Go find me witches," she whispered to the man. "Make them mine. Use the nerve chewers in your case."

"I will."

The microscopic nerve chewers, when injected, would eat their way across the nerve networks of a human and into the brain, and take over most of the personality. Raska preened. This transportable method was her invention. This way, she could stay here safely, and send out her Bak-lal people to convert others.

As the Christopher cleaned off the blood, dressed in its suit, put on shoes, and combed its hair, Raska was already dipping her metal feelers into the internet data stream from which she drank daily. The things she found on there, the things humans said to each other. *Yumm.* She slurped up more data and settled. She twitched her gigantic legs where they extended hundreds of yards into the dirt, her mind plump with gigabytes and YouTube videos, dreaming of victory and of calling to her people.

With one awakened eye, she watched the human. Briefcase in hand, he went to the outer air-locked door and departed for the grueling climb that led to the surface.

Come. Come to me, my sisters and brothers, to Earth, for humans are plentiful and weak, and awaiting our glorious instruction.

Chapter 2

The mission, such as it was, hadn't begun well. Brask had taken him out through the tunnel connecting the ship and the house, then brought him here, to the jetty at the back. The lake was still. Pinpoint lights and chirping from the weed-clogged banks told of bugs exploring the night. Brask handed him what he remembered was called a fishing rod then Brask proceeded to fiddle with his own rod, put bait on a hook, and cast the line out across the dark water.

Stom frowned and stared at the rod and the line dipping into the lake. Frivolous. And it reminded him of home, as did the light of the fireflies and the trees, the sway of their branches and the murmur as wind ruffled through the leaves.

Difficult to believe that the Preyfinder's massive ship was buried beneath these waters. He heaved out a sigh. Calmness had crept in, no matter how he resisted. This Earth was a world of peace. He bowed his head a little, watching from under his brow, remembering. The moonlight had found its way through leaves and left dapples on the skin of his forearms. The splashes of dark and light matched his Feya coloring – a camouflage pattern of black on paleness. In plain daylight he was as obvious as an Earth zebra on an open plain. Here, beneath trees, was where he belonged.

"I forgot what it was like to sit beneath trees and think of nothing much." He said the words so quietly that maybe only a mouse would hear him.

"Better?" Brask asked.

He turned and cocked his head.

"You looked ready to crack into pieces back at the ship. I thought this might be good. You're from Grearth? Correct?"

He bit back a terse response. The Preyfinders were just soldiers, men, like him, obeying orders. "Yes. I thought we were to start this mission? Catch a girl, try to make her a pet?"

Silence.

"I've been rewarded for valor." He put aside his fishing rod. "I don't want this. Let's make it fast so I can get off this planet and back doing my job. What's the minimum I can get away with without upsetting anyone?"

Brask chuckled. "You don't want this?"

"I watched my planet burn, break up. I lost my offspring and my bond mate…" He paused, couldn't say her name even now, not without pain. "I don't want another to take her place, not even a pet."

"I understand." Brask began reeling in the line. "I know who you are. I respect you and what you've done. Still, you're the only man who has ever wanted to refuse this, and if you did, you'd make someone higher up panic and pop an eyeball."

"I know. Feya and Igrakk diplomacy is a nightmare."

"The minimum would be this first stage. Studies showed you don't have to have intercourse to transfer the first dose of the pet nano-chem. Kiss her. After that, I'll fudge the figures."

"I'll be done? No hunt?"

"We'll come out and pretend you tried for the second stage of the capture." Brask turned to him. "I'm not making a hero of Grearth do anything he doesn't want to, Stom."

"I might need your team of Preyfinders to cover for me. I'm going to kiss her even if I have a few witnesses."

"Sure." He nodded then rose to his feet and held out his clenched fist. The moonlight reflecting off the lake water played on the blue of his cheek grooves and highlighted the spikes of his hair. "Just make sure it's only a few. We can clean their memories with the *look*, but if you do it in front of too many, questions will be asked."

Stom hauled himself to his feet and knocked his fist against Brask's. "I will do that. And I thank you."

As he collected the rods at their feet, Brask added, "Not that I wouldn't leap at the chance to hunt here myself. In human words, damn, she's hot. Not your girl, another one."

He laughed. It felt surprisingly good and he realized it had been months since he'd even smiled. "Hot? You must show me her."

"Can't. She's gone back to her home city. It's only a dream. Preyfinders never get honors like this. Unless you're lucky, like Jadd. I will survive. Good to see you've at least learned the local Australian language."

"It was simple. Forced language acquisition is nothing compared to weapons training. Some words will come to me as I speak."

"As long as you know 'ass', 'hot', 'cunt', 'fuck', 'where's the nearest toilet', and 'where will this bus take me to', you're good to go."

Stom nodded, sure he was being taunted. "I see. I know those. Except the bus one."

"Pussy? You know 'pussy'? Not the cat variety. Jadd didn't, so maybe the language misses that one?"

"I know it, soldier, but I won't be going anywhere near one of those."

He snorted, grinned. "Come. Let's do this." Then he turned and walked up toward the house, throwing back one last line. "Just don't try to get acquainted by saying, 'is your pussy glowing for me'. Jadd told me that don't work!"

Stom smiled, shaking his head, but he stayed where he was for a while longer.

Was he being terrible by dismissing this reward so lightly? Perhaps. But the sorrow within had already returned. He had no room for anything but this cold grayness and the blood of battle. The light had left his world forever when Nasskia died.

*****

The pub, as it was termed, was thriving with humans – at least twenty were in range. Stom folded his arms and glowered at a girl who ventured into their alcove looking for empty glasses. When they had arrived, despite their concealing long coats, his coloring and height had made several patrons turn and stare. But it seemed even he became a part of the scenery with time.

"They've forgotten me. I'm disappointed." He shifted on the seat, stretched his legs out, and tried not to knock over the opposite chair, again. "Seems we are inconspicuous, even though I have striped skin."

Brask's lip twitched in a half-smile. "You're cuter than most of these. Besides the male with his hair threaded with skulls, tattoos of flames down his neck, and the arsenal of pointy things shoved through lip, nose, and ear, is far scarier. Your black spotty skin is nothing."

Spotty? He raised a skeptical eyebrow at Brask but refused to respond to the good-humored insult.

He and Brask sat at a table in the darkest corner, behind a flimsy screen of plants. The man mentioned was on the other side of the plants with another hulking male. That one had settled for the prettiness of tying his blond hair in a braid. He made mocking comments about every woman who passed nearby.

"This person I'm to kiss, where is sh –"

A woman entered from the left then detoured for the other woman serving customers at the bar. She leaned over, facing away from him, her little black shorts creeping up her bottom and showing off a glimpse of curve, a hint of places no man was allowed to see unless she allowed them.

For a second, he wanted to be one of those men. And if she didn't allow him, he'd...

His throat tightened.

"There." Brask straightened, standing slowly. "Target acquired, as the humans say in the movies." Brask and his obsession with human movies. "She must have been serving at the other bar. I'll leave you to it. Remember. Be inconspicuous. Don't make any move unless you have six or less people in range. We can clean up that many. More is…human word." He clicked his fingers. "…is a bitch. Yes. That."

He was so busy staring at her, he almost missed Brask moving away. "Wait!"

"What? I can't assist you from here on. This has to be your capture. Rules of the game. We just clean up the mess if you expose your alienness too much. And I don't mean sticking your cock out and waving it about."

Stom ignored the crudity. Obviously Brask had been on planet for too long. "This must be false. I thought she was about to die?"

Brask glanced over at the woman who was currently jumping up and down on one shoe heel and waggling her ass while she chatted and unloaded a tray on the counter. "Her? Willow? Yes."

He sat forward and squinted, even though his vision was perfect. Stom waved his hand in Willow's direction. "She's healthy. Perfectly. And are those clothes legal?"

"What?" Brask stepped back to him and leaned over the table. "She's got early Aids with an incurable variety that humans have no idea even exists. Hepatitis from a needle puncturing through her shoe on a run – she didn't even know she did that one – and a local law breaker called Kasper is planning to murder her, possibly even torture her on the way to killing her. Is that good enough for you? It is on her file. We sample billions of medical reports, put them through an AI filter to find things human doctors miss. Then we do recon on the promising ones." He smirked. "And yes, thank the gods, her clothes are legal here."

Ice washed through Stom and cracked into pieces. His mind went blank for a few seconds. Slowly he sat back until the leather upholstery of the seat back squashed under him and creaked. "I didn't read it. The report. I thought the picture must be old. She's…" He couldn't lie. "Beautiful."

"Yes. It's unfortunate but we can't be curing every human of every disease they have. If you decided to win her, we cure her, we rescue her. Otherwise, no."

He looked up and saw the worried expression on Brask's face. The lines on his forehead deepened. He was disturbing this Igrakk warrior? He shouldn't be. Flip-flopping at the first sign of something unexpected, that she was an attractive creature…one he could claim as his pet, that was not the sign of a man with moral boundaries. *She's not mine.*

"I understand."

"Good. And good luck, even if you decide to follow through after all. Especially if you do."

He sensed Brask moving away but couldn't take his eyes off the woman. So sad. Was he going to let her die? No one would replace Nasskia. It would be sacrilege. There were millions upon millions of dying humans. One more meant nothing. Surely?

Over the next hour or two, he stayed where he was, obeying Brask's instructions, watching her as she served drinks and cleaned tables on the other side of the room. It wasn't until late, after the first girl left, that she came his way, and encountered the two men at the nearby table. The blond one chuckled when she picked up the glasses on their table then wiped the table down with a cloth.

The skull-headed one leaned back and ogled her cleavage. "Hey, Willow, how about you come visit me and Turf here after closing? Out back in the car park." He grinned. "It's your lucky night."

She picked up the last glass and barely gave them a glance before weaving her way back to the bar.

The men laughed gruffly.

"Bitch. She looks like she'd eat you up, Turf, man."

Blond-haired Turf squirmed his jeans-clad butt on his chair then swigged down more of his new glass of beer. "Yeah, she will. I'm gonna make sure she chokes on my cock until she's purple."

"Aww. Gee. You're such a sweet guy. I might give her an ass fuck while you do that. Bet she's fuckin' tight. Her and that weird cousin of hers haven't had dick for years."

Stom tried not to break the edge of the table where he held it. Kiss her. That was it. Mission done.

I'm not interfering in her affairs.

After half an hour or so, the two men left and he relaxed a little. Maybe they were merely boasting and nothing to do with this fate of hers? Aids could take many years to kill. A half hour later, it was closing time and a man came in and spoke to Willow. She promptly tidied up a little then headed out the back, through a door behind the bar.

He'd follow after a few minutes, see where she went. Then his warrior-enhanced hearing picked up a small shriek, far away, but close enough to be just outside this building.

Her.

As he ran for the door behind the bar, hurdling the counter and sweeping glasses and bottles to the floor with the tail of his coat, he left behind a thunder of smashing glass. People yelled for him to stop. But out of all this, apart from his anxiety over her safety, his one other concern was that he'd recognized that cry. Anyone else he'd seen here tonight could sing an entire song and he'd not know who it was.

Why was this so?

Be inconspicuous? So he guessed that meant he shouldn't use the twin 357 Magnums he wore in double underarm holsters, or the sub-compact Heckler & Koch MP5 slung at his back beneath the coat, or the… Pity. He could make such a mess with all these neat human weapons.

On his way through the kitchen, he snatched up a bunch of knives and forks and stuck them into a pocket.

He thrust open the back door and counted back the number of spectators he'd run past. Five, minus whoever was outside. It would do. He could hear the two men somewhere around the corner murmuring threats at Willow. He growled and stalked forward. If he killed these two, maybe that meant he didn't have to count them?

The brick wall of the pub dog-legged to the right and he followed it into a short alley. At the far end, past a half-open dumpster, was a quiet street with a warehouse and a few cars. One insect-shrouded streetlight shed meager light. He kept going past the dumpster and found them.

They had her backed into a double door, with Turf holding her wrists above her head. Skull-head had his palm over her mouth and was shoving her T-shirt up above her bra. She was trying to kick them and screaming muffled curses. The man removed his palm from her face long enough to slap her hard, once.

A rage like he'd not felt for eons shrieked in and tore his notions of serenity into scrap-sized pieces.

Before the sound of the slap died away, Stom retrieved the bunch of knives and forks from his pocket. The metal dug its edges into the taut muscles and tendons of his fist. Upon reaching Skull-head, he gave the man a slap that flung him sideways and backward. Stom didn't bother checking where he went, registering his likely destination by the scrape of his clothes sliding on the road, by his yelps, and by the thump and clang as he collided with something metal.

Which left Turf. The man gaped, swinging his head to zero in on this new intruder.

Without hesitating, Stom wrenched away the chunky hand pinning Willow's wrists and sank a fork, then a knife, into Turf's hand between the long rows of bones. He knew where the bones were, and the gaps, and planned to tack him to the wall. It was satisfying to see the silver tines sink in, moistly crackling through sinew and flesh, and vanish, then feel the hard resistance of the timber beneath.

Turf whined and gasped staccato in disbelief. He tugged to free his hand, but stopped at once, shuddering.

Done. He stepped away and stooped to look at Willow.

Though she'd slumped to the ground, she stirred, her hand reaching beneath her as she attempted to rise. A noise alerted Stom. The second man, Skull-head, came charging back.

"You again." He side-stepped and grabbed the man's hair, bringing him to an abrupt halt and hauling him up off the ground, feet dangling.

"Hey!" Skull-head screeched and clutched frantically, trying to free his hair. "Lemme go! Lemme –"

"Quiet! Now. I can't shoot you with this…" Stom pulled the 357 Magnum from its holster. For two seconds he waggled it under the man's nose then slid it away again like a snake vanishing into a burrow. "But you need to learn manners."

A quick feel revealed a knife and a pistol, both of which he threw onto a nearby roof. If Skull-head had used those, it would have been more dangerous. He was being lax and should've searched him, or incapacitated him.

The other one? Stom ground his teeth. With his free hand he patted down the second man and removed another gun.

Turf only whimpered and picked at the firmly embedded fork and knife. The faint light showed blood blurring the silver of the handle, dripping to the earth.

Good. He relished the chance of battle, needed it to quench this rage, even if this was poor opposition.

"You." He tossed Skull-head into the wall, stunning him. "Can join your friend."

It didn't take long. He used up the rest of the cutlery to attach this second man to the timber door. *Thunk, thunk, thunk.* What a nice word, *cutlery*.

He ignored the screams.

With three knives and forks in each palm and one fork in an ear, the man was well skewered beside his partner.

"Don't go anywhere, will you?" Had he just used sarcasm? An odd form of human humor. Brask seemed to have figured it out and was going native to a fair degree. In the human movies Brask watched, the hero always left with a scary, significant phrase.

Stom thought a second then leaned in. "Well, punk. Bet you're wondering if that was six forks or five?"

Apart from gasping, Turf went still, his eyes wide, his left hand ceasing to pluck at the bloodied fork nailing his palm to the door. "What the fuck?"

Skull-head just whimpered.

Willow giggled a little insanely. "You're crazy."

He tsked and straightened. Maybe he should stick to violence.

He helped Willow to her feet, and set off down the alley with the girl, this most delectable female, tucked into his side. Her car was out there. Recon had shown it to him, even if he'd barely registered the location.

By the time they reached her vehicle, she was shivering so hard, her legs barely held her up.

"Give me your vehicle keys."

"My c-car keys? No way. I'm fine." But she collapsed back into the side of her car. "Thank you for the help. But… Go!" She fluttered her hand at him.

"Do I frighten you? I don't mean to."

No bag. She must have them in her pocket, which would be in her shorts. He let his gaze travel leisurely downward, ignoring, as much as he could, the flow of her feminine contours.

She slapped a hand over her pocket. "No."

"Give." He beckoned. "There's two ways I can do this. The second way I put my hand in your pocket."

Faint screams reached them from the alley and she switched her gaze to look past his shoulder. "I don't know you. Maybe you're one of them too. I should call the cops."

"Me? I injured them badly. I'm not with them. You're not thinking clearly. This Kasper will not approve of me." He guessed, took a chance. "If you involve your police, it will make you a worse person in his eyes and you're already in trouble."

The local police were not a good option. He sighed and reached for her.

The loud, hard slap of her hand on his surprised him. She dared?

"Wait! You know about him? You?" She studied him from waist upward, swallowing, shaking her head as if not sure of what she saw, her neck going back and up to encompass his height. "You're big…and your weird tattoos. Shit."

"True. I am large."

Again, she giggled. Cute. The men's noises of distress cut off. From his ear comm he knew it was the Preyfinders cleaning up, memory wiping. Soon, no human but Willow would recall what had happened.

"Where are the cops? Someone must have called them by now with all the crashing and screaming?"

He shook his head. "Maybe they've been freed? Decide. Make your choice. Give."

"No," she whispered. "Couldn't be. 'Sides, I'm not shaking much anymore. I can –"

Stubborn female. He was to kiss her? Not here though, not now, not with blood on his hand. He also had this consuming urge to see her home safely. *Kak.* "Give me them!"

"Okay! Shit. Knickers in a twist, much?" She wriggled her hand into her pocket, pulled out a set of keys, and tossed them to him.

He went through the vehicle usage manual in his head and recalled the simulator training. Then he unlocked the car, ushered her in, and started the engine.

All went well until he rammed into the car parked in front.

"Crap!" Willow squeaked. "Lemme drive!"

"No. I'm competent. The accelerator calibration was off." He managed to reverse and steer out onto the road despite her muttered curses about insurance. *Keep to the left. Left.* This continent used the left.

When over halfway to her place, she sat up. "How do you know where I live?"

He glanced over. "Intuition."

"Guys have that? God damn. Why did I just get in my car with you? How many women have you murdered today?"

Sarcasm time? He had an urge to impress her. "Three?"

Even in the wash of passing street lights, he could see she'd gone pale.

Emergency reverse tactics. "I meant none. I've killed *zero* women today. I was making a joke."

"Fuck." Willow put her hand on her chest. "It's still beating. I'm fine. Only zero today? Let me give you a hint. Three is doable. Next time say fourteen, so I know it's a joke." She cleared her throat. "I need you to tell me the truth about all this. You rescued me, so I'm giving you points for that. But there's something going on here, obviously."

"There is." He nodded. "I'll tell you. When we get to your house."

"Okay. I guess. Are you foreign? That accent sounds kind of Russian. Crap. I should have expected that joke from you after what happened back there."

Her voice dropped a few octaves. "Was that five forks or six, punk. You feeling lucky? Jeez. From *Dirty Harry*, right?" She turned to him and said, her head shaking a little. "Did I really see you take out two of Kasper's idiots with a set of dinner table knives and forks?"

"Yes."

He glanced over. The light silvered her, worshipping the undulations of her body – the upper curves of her breasts where they spilled from the neckline of her T-shirt, her lips, her cheekbones, the sweet curls of her black hair as it frothed around her ears. She was, he fumbled for the as yet unused human word…dead sexy. Hot. Willow was someone he'd like to handle for more than just for a kiss.

Behave. I'm spoken for. Nasskia was his only. His one. Always. He clenched the steering wheel tighter. Do the mission.

The small vial with the pet-creating nano-chem was in his upper pocket.

The things he did to avoid causing a diplomatic fuss.

Instructions: Coat lips. Kiss her or insert the moistened finger into her mouth.

Contacting her oral tissues was all it took, according to Brask. Insert his fingers between her lips. Make her little warm tongue lick over his fingers, between them. Make her suck on them.

He sighed. *Make?* When had he ever made Nassia do anything? They'd been equals. And yet, the idea of making Willow do things invaded his mind.

No. Uh-uh. No.

Almost there. He swung up onto the driveway, cruised along beside a low fence, and braked, switched off the engine. Composed himself. He needed to get his stiff cock into a better place.

Like maybe inside her?

She chuckled, hiccupping. "I just figured it out. You…you knifed and forked them, didn't you? Ohmigod. Oh my freakin god."

"Hmm."

How was he going to do this? There must be a way. Perhaps it was some loss in translation between their separate races? Did humans laugh when worried? She was in extreme trouble and seemed not to understand. Those men had wanted her dead, after they'd taken pleasure from her.

A kiss, a kiss, and only a kiss. The words ran through his mind like water leaping down rapids.

Just a simple kiss, to begin the process. Over the next day, she would change. She'd become aroused, intensely so, when he…*if* he went near her.

But how could he save her from death?

Perhaps he couldn't. Everyone dies. Some sooner than others.

"Sorry," she whispered. "I'm a bit on edge here. You said you'd tell me what's going on."

He eyed her, took in the tenseness of her face. "Can we sit over there?" He pointed toward the door of her house.

"Outside? Sure. I'm not going to invite you in though. On the porch, sure."

And that was how they ended up sitting side by side at the top of the flight of five timber steps, looking out over the white fence. The little street was deserted. The scent of some sweet blossoms drifted in, yet he could still smell Willow. He could feel the need to take her in his arms, comfort her then, yes, kiss her. Do more if his cock had any say in it.

One of the miracles of the universe was that every discovered intelligent race had been mammalian, humanoid, and sexually compatible. There was something to be said for the theory that all intelligence descended from some common stock.

He shook his head.

This wasn't how it was supposed to be.

Before exiting the car, he'd covertly rubbed some of the nano-chem on his lips and gums. He leaned his forearms on his knees and looked over at her. She seemed relaxed, as if being at home made her safer.

"You can take off your coat if you want. I mean… You don't *have* to. It's a hot summer night, is all. Wow. I sound like I'm about to break into song."

He hesitated.

"I'm not trying to seduce you or anything, Mister… What *is* your name? Eh. I'll shut up now. Tell me what all that, back there, was about."

Then he took off his coat, revealing the guns, and watched her catalogue his weaponry.

"Holee shit. *None* of that is legal. Not even the body underneath, I think. Are you like SWAT team or something? I'm pretty sure I should be screaming and running away. You're a mean-looking, mother of a fucking huge guy."

He grunted. How was he a mother?

"You can't deny that. But, somehow I trust you." She shrugged. "Just don't make me look stupid by killing me, please."

"I won't." He smiled. "You want to know all about me."

"Yes."

He took a deep breath.

Chapter 3

She'd been babbling. Willow put her hands between her knees for a moment and squeezed in, trying to find rock steady ground in her head. Whoever this man was, he'd risked something helping her. Maybe not as much as she'd first thought, but something. Injury at least. Crap, he had enough weaponry to start a small war. Once upon a time, before work took over, Nicolai and her had talked about guns. Those were 357 Magnums.

And she still didn't know why she felt okay, even safe, next to him.

In the minimal light from her new porch light, which had turned out the wrong wattage, his tattoos seemed too perfect. The black patterns on his exposed neck, forearms, and face looked natural and even ran up into his short, dark hair. A red curling tat, that looked done over a deeply scarred groove, peeked from under the sleeve of his dark T-shirt.

With the coat off, his build was even more awesome than she'd imagined. His arm and shoulder muscles slid powerfully whenever he shifted – heavy biceps, a neck that looked biteable but not thick. She didn't even *like* superfit guys; they were pure narcissistic assholes most of the time and spent more time preening themselves than a cat.

And yet, next to him, she felt so like a woman. Like he might, any second, reach over, pull her close, and kiss her.

Fuck. Simmer down, hormones.

She let out a long breath and listened to the breeze playing with the gum tree foliage overhead, wondering when he was going to start explaining. This had to be some doozy of an explanation coming. She plucked at her bright pink top. *Scherazade Bar and Dining* ran in curly writing across the breast area.

From what Amy had said, he'd sat at the pub for hours. Seemingly waiting. Barely drinking.

"Cat got your tongue?"

"I'm thinking," he said. "Where to begin."

"Can you tell me your name to start with? I'm Will."

"I thought it was Willow?"

"Uhh, those other two used that, didn't they? They aren't exactly friends. I go by Will. Left Willow behind years ago." When she had to be tough. After her aunt died.

"Why?"

She frowned, unsure if she should tell this stranger. "Willow sounded fragile. That's not me."

He pursed his lips. They were nice manly lips. Kissable. Lickable. *Note: Stop obsessing about this guy.*

"I like Willow. It's pretty. I'm going to call you that. I am Stom."

"Uhh." Her mouth stayed open. Was it rude if she told him not to? Maybe later. Wasn't as if he'd be sticking around.

Stom was an unusual name. Solid though, like him.

Only a few minutes ago, she'd been assaulted. Her throat and face hurt, her wrists too. Maybe she'd have bruises, but…she sniffed…she'd not let it get to her. Bastards.

"Thank you, Stom. I never said thank you for saving me."

"I was glad I could. In fact, if I hadn't saved you…" He clasped his big hands at his front, looked over at her.

What gorgeous eyes he had, for a man. How in hell was she seeing them in the night? They almost glowed. The color entranced her. Aquamarine?

"Yes?" She raised her eyebrows. "If?" She needed to hear this. Hoped it would be something good, like maybe it would offset the evil already done to her tonight.

"If I hadn't, I'd never have forgiven myself. You're a beautiful creature."

Creature?

He nodded as he spoke, as if to convince himself. "I'd have done the same if you'd had an army taking you away. You know you're in danger?"

Oh shit. The warm glow he'd started froze. "What? Well, of course. But I'm hoping you scared them off."

"This isn't a one-off attack. This man, this law-breaker, Kasper, he wants to kill you and probably torture you badly first."

After a few seconds, she managed to squeeze out some words. "What do you mean? How do you know this?" Fear was trying to shut her down. Not. Happening. She had Ally to look after.

"I know this because I'm an alien from another planet. You've been chosen as a special subject and have been watched and studied. It's fact."

His words went a long way away. She heard them but they were so nonsensical she didn't comprehend for a few seconds after he said them.

"…and if you don't do something, he will kill you. I have a choice. I'm telling you this so as to get you to run away from here. Go. Soon. Take whatever you can and run."

"What?" She felt her forehead crease, let his last sentence run around in her head again. "Why are you trying to mess with me? Just tell me the truth. I don't think joking is nice or, or anything! Not after what just happened to me."

"Willow –"

"Will. Thank you."

He blinked. "Run. Please. It isn't a joke."

Oh this was just ridiculous. She didn't need this. Besides, she couldn't see why he was doing it. Why help her then tell stupid stories? Was he nuts? Trying to mindfuck her? And with all those guns? Maybe they were toys? They must be.

An image of him stabbing a fork into Turf's hand flashed into her mind but she shoved it away.

She stood. Anger tore her up. The next words blurted out before she could stop herself. "Fuck you."

Ally might be wondering why she was out here. Forget this asshole.

"Wait. Willow." He shot upright and grabbed her hands then added in his rumbly voice that shivered deep inside her, "You need to believe me."

When she tugged and tugged, and couldn't get free, her anger, stupidly, drained away.

He stared down at her like he could drive his words into her very soul. "Believe. You *must* believe me. Run away, fast. Go tomorrow."

She swallowed, petrified, but not of him holding her. The fear was of what he meant, of how he was distorting her reality. Somewhere in what he said, she sensed truth and a world of horrendous and incalculable *wrongness*.

"I can't." Her words sounded so squeaky. "I have Ally. She needs me." Tears wet her eyelids and she trembled. "I can't leave."

It would take her weeks to convince Ally. Months to sell the house. She had no spare cash, nowhere else to go, and why was she even contemplating all this?

Then he leaned in and kissed her. He wrapped his big solid, man-heavy arms around her, fairly crushing her to him, and kissed.

A shudder of lust slammed into her every cell. A volcanic explosion might, barely, have had the same effect. She opened her mouth and found he was already taking advantage of that small concession – nipping, licking and pushing his tongue inward past her lips. His wide thigh had somehow nudged her legs apart. His male scent assaulted her as much as the feel of him taking of her what he wanted.

Goose bumps swept across her skin in a chill wave that seemed to sensitize every tiny hair on her body.

"Stop. Wait," she protested, murmuring around his lips, breathing more of him in, feeling parts of him shift to accommodate her own moves, knowing he was touching her most intimate places.

God. Her clit was pulsing hot against his thigh. She'd wet through her panties for sure. As he pushed on her there, the cloth slid on the moisture.

While he kissed the corner of her lips, he curved her backward. She moaned and squirmed as he explored further down her neck, to the first swell of her breasts, wanting more of him, clutching at his back. His leg ground upward between her legs and she replied, pushing against him, dying to get more, more, more.

Fast, frantic, this was a tsunami of lustful impulses.

Some ecstatic and unmeasured time later, he lowered her to the porch timber and covered her body with his. Clothing was shoved and stretched. His mouth searched for and engulfed her nipple – a shock of wet heat that made her arch and groan. He sucked on her, tongue lapping, rasping at her. Then his hand slid, his fingers rubbed downward over her clit and along her slit. Probing her, pushing inward in the rhythm of sex. His thumb took over the task of massaging her clit. She made some odd choking noise, and pressed her hips upward, straining to get his fingers in her despite the shorts and her panties being in the way.

Should she protest? The idea arrived and was gone in the same instant.

Touch me.

He found a solution, must've pushed aside her underwear. Some part of him thrust into her pussy. Fingers. Fingers shoving in…out, thumb rubbing, circling, rubbing.

She clawed blindly at his hair and his shoulders.

This was insa –

"Oh god. God. Stop." She panted, whimpered, writhed on his hand. "I'm going to…" A climax possessed her, echoing as he kept on playing his tongue over her nipple. She imagined that tongue, those lips, below and had a last exquisite tremor wrack her body.

Spent, gasping, she was vaguely aware of him shifting. She opened her eyes to see him over her, looking down at her with those translucent jewel-blue eyes.

"I think that qualifies as a kiss."

The thickness in her throat made it hard to speak. "God, yes."

What had just happened? Why… Her mind ran off in all directions. Why had she done that? Been so overcome?

"Mmm." He stroked hair from her forehead. "Poor little female. I'm going to solve this problem of yours, somehow. I promise."

For a while she let him caress her then she struggled up onto her elbows. Why had that felt so right? She'd reacted like an animal on heat – disengage brain and engage sex kitten.

And if there was one thing she wasn't, it was a poor little female. Even if he wanted to help her, what a demeaning way to say it. Her eyes narrowed.

"You're going to solve *my* problem?"

"Yes."

"And if I say I don't want your help?" And she wasn't convinced she had a problem.

"Are you?" His hand stilled.

"Maybe."

She shook her head, unsure what she was most disturbed about. He'd told her he was an alien only a few minutes ago. A few lust-crazed minutes ago. Either he was nuts, or not. If he was then her behavior became crazy too. He hadn't drugged her. Though if he were an alien, maybe he had a sex ray or something… And maybe she needed to go swallow some of Ally's pills.

"Did you do something to me, mister?" she asked suspiciously.

"Not yet." He studied her. "Although I like that you ask questions, you need to ask them more…what's the word? It's a type of niceness…"

"Huh. You want more respect?" She arched an eyebrow, aware she was challenging him. Though if he truly was an alien, and not some Russian drug syndicate crim who'd sampled too much of his own smack, maybe he'd not get the subtlety?

Alert. Warning. Nut job in proximity. Why was she even vaguely, with more than half a brain cell, considering he might be an alien? Because he'd just made her melt? Because he acted so solid, down-to-earth and non-fantasy that Tinkerbell's wings would fall off if she was here?

"Respect? Yes. That's it."

Ahh, she couldn't resist. "Twat."

He reached under, fisted her hair, and anchored her to the floor with it. "I know that's an insult."

Her gasped out indignant, "Ow, ow, ow," and her wriggling against his hold, achieved nothing except to make him smile triumphantly.

He waited for her to stop wriggling. "I can see you'd be a constant challenge to any male who claimed you."

"No one's claiming me unless they want their balls on a plate."

"First, I'd have to cut out that adventurous tongue."

She snapped her mouth shut and ventured a frown.

Funny how she'd not told him to fuck off. She really should, except she was too wrapped up in watching him watch her, and seeing the changes on his face. There were differences in his cheek structure, and ears, and other little things like his eyebrow hair growing the wrong way…and did that have to mean he was an alien? Maybe if your eyebrow got shot off it could grow back wrong? Maybe he was just inbred with weird genes? If that were the case, inbred had some big pluses and she wanted to meet his brothers.

Whatever the cause, she figured she could read him. He seemed like a man who'd discovered something that both pleased him and saddened him.

She was also all too aware that this, being held down and examined, was turning her on, immensely so. She kept her legs together and ignored the pulse of blood in her temples and between her legs.

"I have to go."

When he released her, she tried not to look disappointed. When he said a quiet goodbye and walked away from her, down her stairs, and perhaps out of her life, she had to dig her nails into her skin to stop herself calling him back.

Rescue a girl, tell her you're her answer to all her problems then just waltz off without explaining? Didn't the man know date etiquette? Hero etiquette?

She sat up and wrapped her arms around her knees, rustling up some dignity despite everything. One thought kept returning to her – it was good to know someone thought her worth rescuing. She looked out for Ally, tried to save some money for when they'd need it, to get ahead, but the house was in bad need of repairs and the medicine bills climbed over her head. On the days when life was serving up lemons, she wondered if she was worth more than spit.

Her nails were chewed down to nothing. She played with the ragged end of one. Didn't help that she'd almost forever nursed an irrational fear that she'd somehow made her parents die.

Now her alien hunk had deserted her too.

His words came back to her: *You've been watched and studied.*

Creepy and yet strangely reassuring. Should she contact the cops or some alien worshipping society? At least he hadn't probed her yet. Wait, he had. Willow laughed a little crazily.

Fuck this. She shoved back some straying curls and scrambled to her feet. The real world called.

Chapter 4

Mandy wriggled into a better position on the sofa as she knitted the last rows of the tiny green pullover. Then she held it out before her. Her fingers had gone a bit numb from her stupid carpal tunnel problem but this was so worth it. Who would've thought anyone would want pullovers for little oil-slicked penguins? The darn things were such cuties she hadn't been able to resist when she'd seen the link on Facebook for people to knit these to help save them.

Phoebe and Jamie were doing this too. They were racing each other.

She'd begun a second one when the front door opened and clicked shut. His footsteps on the tiles made her grin. What the hell would he think of this latest venture? Being a dentist, he was very practical and no-nonsense.

Her feet jiggled. Hugging and screaming was what she needed to do.

No. She wouldn't get all excited, not yet. She'd pretend nonchalance, despite him being too busy with the conference to do more than text once or twice. Mean man.

His shadow eclipsed the opening to the hall. She flung aside the pullover, leaped up and ran to him, grinning. Fuck being calm, he'd been away days!

"Christopherrr! How was the flight? What was Adelaide like? Why didn't you return calls? You're –"

The blankness on his face chilled her. What was this?

She put a hand out and touched his arm. "What's wrong?"

"Nothing. Come here."

She smiled, tension ebbing, and melted into his embrace. "I missed you so, *so* much."

Then something stung her cheek and she slipped, senseless, into a white oblivion.

When she awoke she found herself tied, spread-eagled, ever so tightly to their big double bed. Naked, she was naked. Mandy licked her dry lips, stumbling inside her mind to make sense of this.

Had she been drinking and forgotten?

When Christopher appeared still dressed in his suit at the periphery of her vision, she turned her head and smiled shakily. He'd never been kinky.

Something metal and silvery glinted in his hand.

"Chris? Baby? What are you doing?"

Wordless, he approached and raised what she recognized as one of his dental implements to her wrist.

"Chris! Hey! Stop that!" She twisted her body, cringing away as the drill screamed into its little metal whine. She remembered him telling her once that the motor inside it could spin the end drill six bazillion times a second or something. Her throat clamped in tight enough to choke her into not breathing. But she couldn't look away, couldn't tear her eyes off the terrifying thing.

She writhed more, helpless to escape but still trying. The sharp point bit her skin, sinking in. Redness spurted and she screamed for all of one second before he planted something over her mouth.

After that she still screamed but the sound was mostly inside her head, muffled, harsh. Even her eyeballs strained with pressure as she threw her head from side to side, as if they would pop from the inside.

He moved on to do her right ankle, having to use his weight to keep her completely still. Then he did her left, then her other wrist, ignoring her whining distress, the arching of her spine, the desperate flinching of her muscles.

Her throat was raw from the screaming.

The *pain*. Her bones jittered when the metal went too deep.

Christopher, her Christopher…this wasn't him, couldn't be. It was some monster. Tears coursed down her face. She fought the urge to throw up.

Who was this man?

After extracting the drill from the flesh of her wrist, he stepped back and watched. The multiple pains throbbed and lanced at her. She blinked away the last of her tears, her chest rising and falling in ragged movements, breathing rasping in her ears. Would the neighbors hear? Would they call the police? They must. They must. Before he did something worse.

Maybe he was done?

Had to be. Had to be. He was done.

Her hopes nearly floated her off the bed. She tugged on the ropes. But no, she was still fastened down, immobile.

Let me go, she pleaded with her eyes, wrinkling her forehead.

Then something twitched inside her, under the skin of her wrist. Cold yet searing hot, as if something tiny was in there. She tried to roll her eyes upward to the headboard, to focus on her outstretched arm, and felt the sensation advance up her arm. She swore she could hear something crunching, could smell the blood, could feel the tearing of her tissue. Minute jaws nibbled on her.

Fuck, fuck. Fuck. Mandy blubbered her fears into the object blocking her mouth, shrieking silently as the small terrible agonies began in her other arm and then her feet.

Though she writhed and nearly tore her arms from their sockets, nothing came loose; her body stayed there, splayed out, blood trickling from the holes. She was being eaten on the inside. Panting wetly past the gag, with the fear clawing at her so hard that red prickled at her eyes, she looked at him.

Christopher's mouth straightened then curved upward and he smiled for the first time.

"Hello, little bitch."

Chapter 5

"Talia!"

She jumped and turned to find Greg, the lab's nice guy, staring at her.

The strange tug on her that made her want to leave ASAP and travel north zipped away. It'd come back, guaranteed. Just like when she woke every morning, she'd recall dreams of a man with water-clear green eyes in a dark swirling coat, and a blood-smeared crazy guy crawling about the walls of Brittany's destroyed apartment.

Her memories of the devastation after the earthquake seemed so odd, and so tainted. Though having your sister declared missing, presumed dead, after a massive disaster might tend to give anyone nightmares.

"You were about to turn into stone if you stood there any longer." He nodded at her coffee mug. "And the spoon may have dissolved."

She twitched the corner of her mouth as she lifted the teaspoon out. "With the disgusting brand they buy for the staff room, I wouldn't be surprised."

"It is pretty toxic. I'm on my third stomach transplant this year." He slumped into one of the armchairs around the coffee table. "Lucky you're off on sabbatical tomorrow. While you're out in the big normal world, drink some good coffee and tell me what it's like." He paused. "Are you okay? You look shaky."

"I'm fine. I think lunch disagreed with me."

It was him, though. The mystery man. She knew exactly what she'd find at the end of the journey her urge was pulling her to take. Not the bloodied man, not some revelation about Brit's apartment, *him*, the man in the coat. Was it from sneaky hypnosis, or a psychosis, something she needed therapy for? Before she hired a shrink she was going to go back to Brisbane to see if she could find that elusive clue that would explain everything.

Oh hell, who was she fooling? She needed to go back there to find him…if he existed, and she knew he did, which was just not logical. And if she did find him, she was going to yell at him for giving her insomnia for months. Bastard. Whoever he was.

Pity she couldn't take a sword on the plane. That was the other half of the urge – go armed. There was something, or someone, bad, waiting for her too. Anyone sensible would want to carry a gun, and there was her insane urge again. *Sword, sword, sword*, it whispered to her.

"What's that?" Greg stood at her shoulder. "Hey, great origami kite."

"Yeah." Talia ran her finger over the folds. It was a paper sword, only she wasn't telling him that. Her origami truly sucked.

"Make sure you relax in between studying. I need you back again in a few months ready to teach and finish off that thesis."

"Definitely. The University of Queensland looks fantastic but the beaches there are as good as they get. I'll bring you back loads of pictures of surf, sand, and swimsuits."

And men with swords, and creepy wall-climbing guys.

"Ssss!" She sucked on her finger where blood welled from a paper cut.

The red on her pale skin was alarming. The droplet on the paper looked frightening. She was fine with blood when it was in a pipette, but not like this – fresh and raw. If she ever got to really use a sword on someone, she'd likely faint.

Chapter 6

"Willow?"

Someone shook her. No one called her that anymore, except for him. Alarmed, she blearily opened her eyes. "Ally!" She smiled at her cousin. "Just you."

The morning light streamed in through the window and silhouetted Ally. As she leaned in, wisps of her long hair shifted against the glaring white. White on white. No one had blond hair as pale as Ally's. "Yes, just me. I was worried. It's late."

"What time?" Her arm ached when she turned to see the clock. She hissed. Also hurting was her neck.

"It's nine. You've got bruises, Willow."

"Will. Remember? Willow isn't me anymore."

"No. I've decided I like it again."

"You've decided?" *Shit.* The little frown on Ally's face said she wasn't changing her mind. When her cousin got an idea, it stayed got.

"I've made you coffee. It's in the kitchen."

"Thanks." She was such a sweet thing. "I'll be up in a few minutes."

"No, you won't." Ally stood, *determined* written all over her face. "Turn over. I'm going to massage you. It'll make you feel better."

Though she considered protesting, she gave up and rolled over, sighing when Ally's long fingers began their work. The girl knew how to fix muscle aches like no one else.

Willow now, hey? She played with the syllables in her mind. Funny how she had two people wanting to use the old name. Maybe it wasn't such a bad idea? It was pretty. She didn't need the name change to prove her toughness anymore.

Ally's fingers reached a knot high on her shoulder and she groaned in relief as the pain ebbed.

"I hit the right spot?"

"Yes. Wonderful." She tucked her head deeper into her pillow.

"What happened?"

Oops. How much could she say? She didn't want to upset her. Ally was so innocent of the outside world. She received a government payment for looking after her and that, with her wages, helped them both keep the house, pay rates, live. But there wasn't anything that could make Ally lose her fear of what was out there. People scared her to bits. Crowds ditto and parks and open spaces in the city. Open spaces in the country were strangely okay; the one time she'd tried taking her camping had proved that. But they couldn't afford to go camp out in the middle of nowhere forever.

Her psychiatrist had resorted to drugs and a few checkups a year, once it was clear they couldn't afford expensive treatment.

"Who gave you these marks?" Her delicate fingers trailed cool and comforting over Willow's neck. "It wasn't the man who came to our door, I know that."

"What?" She turned back over and sat up.

Ally shifted down the bed and waited, wide-eyed, her hands curled in the lap of her green dress, and looking like some ethereal creature who'd been caught casting a spell.

"How'd you know about him, about Stom?"

She sucked on her lip for a moment or two. "He's different, isn't he?"

"You saw him through the front window?"

"No. I heard you talking, just a little. Then I went back to sleep once I knew he was safe. He likes you."

Every so often Ally surprised her with some conclusion that didn't seem possible. Willow sat back against the headboard. "Likes?"

She thought about that. He had saved her from rape and assault, told her he wanted to rescue her from evil, and given her a great orgasm. *Likes* summed it up, pretty much. Then he'd hinted at claiming her, ohmigod.

Ally poked out her tongue. "Was I right?"

"Little smartass."

"See! Come get coffee and tell me about your new boyfriend." Then she bounced upright and pranced down the hallway. "I like him too!" she tossed back.

Willow rotated her head, testing her muscles. Her back and everywhere felt so much better. The girl had magic in those fingers.

It wasn't until she'd eaten a bowl of cereal and had a second mug of coffee under her nose that Ally gave her the eye. "What?"

"Him. Tell me. Please? And the other stuff. I need to know what happened last night."

Their little house was flanked by the culvert with the jungle of vines and overgrown shrubbery on one side, and the furniture warehouse on the other. The neighbors across the road had their nights of drag racing and loud music, but really, her aunt had lucked out. They were a fortress of isolation. The crime rate was high enough, around here, that if you had the same door lock for more than a year, you went and bought a lottery ticket. Or stole one.

"I don't think you need to know, Ally," she said quietly.

"I do." Pale of face, yet resolute, the girl clutched her coffee mug. "I think I do."

Damn. She swallowed a mouthful of lukewarm yet super-strong coffee.

Lucky? In fifteen years, they'd never had a burglary. The one time someone had rocked the roof, they'd screamed and run off before she'd wrenched the door open to yell at them. This place was safe. How could she tell Ally about last night when she was so naïve? Nothing bad got into this house. Not since she came to live here, after her parents died in the fire.

She shut her eyes, hiding the pain. The memory of that still hurt like nothing else ever would.

"It's okay, Willow. I'll protect you."

The sadness in her voice made Willow open her eyes and smile. "Course you will."

"But you *have* to tell me. I promise you, I will worry more if you don't tell me."

Such big, earnest, gray eyes. It was possibly true. Ally fluctuated from mood to mood. She already was worried.

Willow sighed. She tapped the mug then sat forward to hunch over it. "Fine. What happened… Some men tried to attack me after work, at the pub." And she hadn't called the cops either. She glanced up but Ally only nodded.

"The man you heard, he rescued me. He was like a knight in shining armor, galloped in, beat up the bad guys, brought me home. But he says he's an alien. Clearly he's insane. Says I'm being studied and that he's going to fix my every problem." She chuckled and shook her head, took another sip.

"Uh-huh." Ally looked serious, lifting and lowering one eyebrow then the other like she did when she was thinking. "Sounds cool. If you don't want him, I'll have him."

Mouth open, she stared back. What the? The girl had never said anything like that about her other boyfriends. "He says he's an alien!"

"So?" She shrugged. "Minor deet."

"Minor fucking detail! What?"

"Shhh." She waved her hand downward. "Stop shouting. So, did you do it?"

"I…what? Did I do what?" But they both knew. Somehow she knew that Ally, smug girl who never left the house unless the sky was falling, knew he'd done something intimate to her. "Um. No." Hell if she was going to say it out loud.

"Okay." Then she took a macaroon from the packet in the middle of the table and bit down. The crunching filled the awkward silence. Willow could swear she was smirking.

The subject of their discussion surfaced in her head. All confident and male, a man who had possibly made her come in record time. They'd clicked, at least sexually. Even now, her pussy awakened, warmth spreading. Where his fingers had been, the places he'd touched, she seemed to feel his skin against her again, even up inside her, as if she'd ever forget that invasion. That had been so hot.

The clink of china jolted her from her reverie. Ally was washing up and she hadn't noticed her stand or push back the chair. She had her back turned. Furtively, Willow pressed the heel of her hand to her groin and inhaled sharply, biting back a moan. She was going to have to unearth her vibe from her underwear drawer ASAP.

"If you want to date him, I'm fine with that. Even if he is an alien."

She raised an eyebrow. "I'm not sure I should thank you for that. Besides, he mightn't be my type."

"He is. He's a good alien. Pass me your mug."

She stretched and did so. "Meaning there's bad aliens up there too?"

"Oh sure there are. Only some are down here."

A chill crept in, like something dark and insectile crawling through her on little cold feet. Ally said the oddest things sometimes. Tomorrow, or even this afternoon, she'd be biting her nails and hiding under the bed sheets again. Least she hadn't told her about Kasper being involved. That would definitely have freaked her out more than a fantasy alien.

Her next shift at the hotel was evening again, starting at four o'clock. She phoned, bracing herself for questions, though also wondering why she'd not heard from the cops. How could that disturbance not have been reported to them by *someone*?

There was nothing. When she begged off her shift due to being assaulted, Cheri was appalled, shocked, sympathetic – everything except aware that it had happened a few yards from the back door of the hotel.

How could this be? Sure, Stom had suggested things had been cleaned up somehow but she hadn't believed it.

This wasn't simply a matter of Kasper buying silence with threats. Cheri didn't know anything at all about anything.

Even all the breakages – yes, she'd heard the glass shattering from the alley – but it was dismissed as a drunken brawl. After assuring Cheri that she'd call the police about the assault, Willow said goodbye.

Was any of what Stom had said true? How? How could it be? Yet what else could explain people plain missing memories like that? It made her think.

She stood in front of the bathroom mirror, in her underwear, poking her injuries and trying to decide if she was going crazy, or if it was Stom who was, or maybe the rest of the world.

The bruises on her neck were in the shape of fingers.

"What if no one is crazy?" she whispered. If it were true…she stared down at the soap next to the basin. The one thing she remembered so well it was seared into her mind, was when he'd finger-fucked her.

Her boyfriends in the past, some had been handsome, some too pretty for their own good, but only Stom was so massive, so daunting.

What was with that? He could've snapped her like a…she prodded her electric toothbrush…like a toothbrush, but he hadn't. He'd sat there on the step, talked, and when she tried to run away, he'd grabbed her to make his point, and kissed her.

The memory was fresh and she could feel his tongue on her nipple. The little bumps around the edge of her areola rose up as she watched herself, remembering the roughness yet also the softness of his tongue on her, lapping, wet, hot. She whimpered and reached blindly for the toothbrush. She'd never tried it before but the thing buzzed and she was rather desperate. The bedroom was too far away.

Ally was watching TV from the sounds coming from the living room.

She switched it on, slowly approached the front of her panties where her clit was already poking up in a little bulge against the lace. Before it even contacted her, she held her breath, anticipating. She moved it that last half inch, touched. Oh my. She gasped and crumpled forward.

She ran the head of the buzzing device up and down, pressing the material into her slit before returning to the ultimate destination, her feral, throbbing, upstanding clit that was damn near screaming out to be touched.

Using an electric toothbrush – so slutty, so gorgeously nice.

Buzz. Buzz.

Pleasure swamped her in waves of fucking awesomeness. Her nipples begged to be touched too, standing up and aching. She eyed herself. She wasn't the biggest girl in the boob department, but maybe she could reach herself?

Still rubbing the plastic back of the toothbrush on exactly that right spot on her clit that aroused without being too much, she pressed her left breast upward and stretched, straining to lick herself. The tip of her wet tongue made the distance, just. She circled the nipple, dabbing, tapping, feeling the sensations meet and intermingle.

She bucked forward onto the toothbrush.

"Ohh, fuck."

Though her neck hurt she kept up the exquisite double act, her hand half-circling her breast while the delicious buzz throbbed and hummed into her pussy. She panted, licking, feeling the sensations build. At last, straining forward with her thighs, and writhing a little on that naughty vibrating thing, she came. She shuddered, gasping through the orgasm, half-conscious she might be overheard.

"Fuck, fuck, fuck." Her legs gave out and she kneeled on the bath mat, with her forehead on the cool painted timber, and the toothbrush still rattling away.

"Well," she mumbled, switching it off with her thumb. "Fun."

How decadent. The crotch of her panties felt slippery with her moisture. She very carefully cleaned her toothbrush, glad she hadn't succumbed and tried to put it inside her. That would be so slutty, so bad, so disgusting. But she had thought it for a second or two.

At least now she had it out of her system. An orgasm a day keeps the mind from wandering. Damn, it was hot in the bathroom.

Hot, oh yes. Stom was that by far.

Already she had ideas. If he'd been here, right now, she'd have jumped him. Alien nutter story or not.

Embarrassing.

Think work. She had the firefighter training run in a few days. Tomorrow she'd have a go at jogging over the course. She'd be well enough by then. There weren't going to be that many chances to get into the next trainee firefighter intake and all this strangeness wasn't going to stop her.

Willow fanned herself. Her face was flushed. Maybe she should wait before going out where Ally could see her.

Maybe she could try the toothbrush again to see if she could do it twice?

She switched it on, feeling even guiltier, but found a second climax elusive. Apart from sending her clit numb, nothing happened.

All that day, she tried, using her fingers and her super-throbby vibe, cursing her horniness and even eventually, the absent Stom. She couldn't, quite, come. So close but no relief arrived.

The inner certainty that Stom could help her go over the edge became such a draw that it sank in and made a light bulb flicker on. He *had* done something to her. Bastard.

How? Not possible.

"Damn." While staring up at the darkened ceiling, she wriggled against her fingers. She needed sleep, and she wasn't getting any – sleep or orgasms.

"Fuck you, Stom. I will not be dictated to." So she rolled over, punched her pillow and shut her eyes, determined to ignore the throb in her groin.

She drifted into sleep, only to dream of sitting atop Stom and slowly sliding down onto his cock. She woke in the middle of that one and lay blearily looking past her forearm at the darkened room, feeling her thoughts assemble.

How dare the man invade her dreams? She closed her eyes and imagined running Stom over with a stampede of baaing sheep. Willow smiled. That helped. She snuggled deeper into the bed.

Morning arrived. She awoke and found herself sweaty and so wrapped in tangled sheets that it took a whole minute to free herself. Her damp underwear had left a wet spot on the sheet and her inner thighs slippery. Yet she remembered nothing of the rest of the night. Dreams were such sneaky things.

Face in hands, Willow sat on the edge of the bed, tired, and still aroused.

She slumped through breakfast, munching corn flakes, raising a brow at the chatter of the overly cheerful Ally. Afterward she ventured out onto the back concrete step, coffee mug in hand, to sit contemplating the gray curve of the concrete reservoir that overshadowed the rear of the house.

This had always been a good place to sit and think. Even Ally liked it out here and on a few occasions, they'd climbed the ladder together to the top of the reservoir. They'd lain up there looking at the sky and the wandering clouds. Brilliant times.

Life had become strange. She'd been meaning to jog today, to keep fit for the firefighter tests, but her brain had kicked back into gear. What the hell had she been thinking? Jogging? Now, when her life was in a mess? Either Stom was an alien, or worse, he was a loony. Either Kasper was after her and aiming to kill her, or he wasn't, and what had happened was an isolated assault.

An isolated assault that no one else had seen or remembered? Which wasn't possible, was it? Where did that leave her?

The sick feeling in her stomach solidified into a lump. She had to sort this out. Either way, Stom was right. She should be running – either from Kasper or from him, or both.

Did aliens exist? She pulled her phone from her pocket and began searching. Google wasn't the be all and end all but it was a beginning.

Are aliens real, she typed.

Could anyone sane be thinking about this question? There was an Australian Cynics Organization or ACO. The cynics were into debunking alien and paranormal theories and sightings. Better to talk to someone who had their feet in the real world, surely? A tiny unpolished website led her to an actual phone number, as well as an email and, what the hell, could it hurt?

Someone answered.

"Hello?"

At the other end of the line was a man who sounded about eighty but after some cautious questions she asked him about aliens and how to tell if she met one. He gave her a whole spiel about higher technology and different bodily appearance and the communication difficulties that would be likely.

"What if they look like us?" she asked.

After a short silence he said what seemed a key point. "Something will be different. The more you look, the more you would find." He paused again. "Why do you think this person is an alien? The simplest explanation for anything is often the correct one. If they've told you they are one, it's likely they're not, but that somehow, that lie helps them. Are they asking for money, personal details? They could be dangerous."

Willow swallowed. Her heart was thumping on her ribs. She could feel it in her neck arteries, in her temples. How had he picked up on the fact that she'd met someone she suspected? She must sound such a doofus.

"He called himself a hunter. He...they, seem to be able to wipe memories."

"Uh-huh. Okay. Then how come you remember him?"

Good point. She slowly lowered the phone to her knee, listening to the distant squawking before pressing *end*.

This was impossible to figure, unless Stom gave her some more clues, and he wasn't here. Maybe he wasn't coming back? Maybe he was the most insane man she'd ever met.

Kasper was real, though. Even if she wasn't on his hit list, she couldn't tell that for sure, and she definitely should do something positive. Dying was hard to come back from. Kasper might not be a psychopath...then again, he might be. She'd heard bad things.

But, leaving here, on a whim? The men who attacked her had said nothing about Kasper being after her.

She put her finger to her mouth and nibbled on the stub of a nail.

They couldn't run, not without Ally being far more prepared.

"So." She squeezed the phone until the edges hurt her hand then did it again, because it made the headache go away. "I guess I need a gun."

Nicolai. Bonus points, he knew people who knew Kasper, and would tell her things if she asked nicely. Probably. Maybe. Gossip might be her savior, even if she dreaded knowing, even if the gossip was bad news.

She dug her nails into her palm. Wanting the pain. The distraction. "I hate this."

Her palm had a row of red crescents.

She wanted to go back to being anonymous, like she'd been most of her life. If this was Kasper's doing, rescuing Monique must have been the catalyst. Had the house failed her or had Kasper been reminded of what had happened by someone in the car? She didn't know the distance the house's effect worked for, only that it did. Unless…it was wearing off?

When she first recognized what was happening, she'd wondered if it might be her aunt's ghost helping them out. If so, would she some day move on and leave them to fend for themselves? And if it was simply the house, why and how?

Aliens weren't that far a stretch when your house might be alive.

The reservoir loomed high above her. By midday it would be radiating heat. You could put your palm on it and be pleasantly warmed on autumn days. You could lean on it and be comforted, like a child cradled by their mother. It was so big, so indestructible, and so *solid*.

She'd be sad to leave here, didn't *want* to leave here.

Like someone stretching out to check their lover was still in bed with them, she placed her hand on the timber of the back porch then heaved in a long breath. This place was in her blood. Most of the years of her life had been lived here. No way was she upping and leaving just 'cause someone told her she should.

Ally came out wearing one of the light summer dresses she favored, sat beside her on the step and said, "You okay?"

The clarity and brightness of Ally's gaze often surprised her.

"Yes." She squeezed Ally's hand. "I'm fine." Telling her about her weird deductions was out, especially about getting a gun, except maybe, just in case they did have to, she had to be told about the move. "We might have to leave the house, for a while. Go stay somewhere else until things settle down. Is there anywhere you want to…"

Her gray eyes widened, alarmed. "No," she whispered, shaking her head. She looked away, down at her knees. "I don't want to leave."

"What if we have to?"

"No." Though she said it sharp as a nail banging into a wall, her voice shook.

"It won't be straight away. I'd have to organize stuff. Ally?"

"I can't. I can't. *I can't!*"

Ignoring her, the girl rose and went back inside, the fly-screen door snapping closed behind her.

"Fuck."

That had gone well.

Willow took a few deep calming breaths then picked up the phone and found Nicolai's number. She was pretty sure she recalled his code for buying off him. He wasn't a man for exchanging long messages on text. A minute later, she had a place to meet and a date to collect the gun. Tomorrow, six am. Two hundred dollars, cash, and that was at a big discount from memory.

The old piggy bank, her purse, the change in the car, and the coins she scrounged from around the house brought her up to being only three dollars short. Going out, weaponless, to visit the ATM made her feel queasy. This would do. It would have to, though they wouldn't be eating much even if she braved the ATM. Not with her not working.

For all her attitude, she was scared. Stom had planted a seed of disturbance. Being beaten while held against a wall by two thugs had a part in that too. Fucking scary. She'd need to be ice woman for that to not bother her.

She piled all the money on the quilt of her bed, spread the coins around. "If I spend this on a gun…" And if it turned out Kasper didn't want to skin her alive after all… Skin her alive, shit, that was a scary thought. Yeah, spend all this and not need the gun? She added in a deadly quiet whisper, "I'd almost be disappointed."

The throb in her groin took her by surprise. Heat. Wetness. Visions of Stom over her, lowering himself, impaling her on his cock.

What. The. Fuck?

She buried her face in her hands but the animalistic need stayed, banging away at her, swelling outward and making all her sexual bits, and then some, drum at her hotly.

Shit. She hurried out and found the lighter in the kitchen drawer then went and sat on the porch again, spent a moment with her fingers pushing onto her pussy through her shorts. Her tight grasp on the lighter dug its plastic edges into her other hand. Such potential there, to defeat this bodily need.

Stom.

Willow groaned softly. This wasn't going away. She didn't need this shit. This ridiculous want, this lust for a man she barely knew.

But she'd not done this for years. The melted scar on her forearm reminded her of why she did this, and yet also, why she mustn't.

She flicked on the lighter. The heat seemed to radiate outward to her eyes…dancing.

Using it beckoned. She hated doing this but the eternal fascination with fire lured her. The sweet flickering yellow and orange.

She held her hand six inches above the fire, three inches, two.

Heat. Flame. The smell brought memories back. Bad ones. She needed this pain, deserved it so much.

A tear blotted onto her forearm then another.

Nothing beat the pain of fire. Nothing. The little tongue curled and strained upward toward her skin.

Lust vanished, hissing into the concentrated heat of the lighter flame licking across the palm of her hand.

Yes.

Oh yes.

Forearm tensed, she screwed up her eyes and let it take her. Stopped. Held her hand out. Did it again.

She deserved this for not saving her parents. Fire had taken them, why not her?

Her sobs were quiet because she didn't want to disturb Ally. This was between her and the fire.

Chapter 7

Stom slammed the heel of his hand into the base of the glass console. "What is she doing? She's burning herself? Gods! And she's getting a weapon? Why isn't she running like I told her to?"

He glared at the one active, glowing square in the long, curved bank. That screen showed the view from the surveillance drone he controlled. The thing was the size of a bug and poised above where Willow sat on the back steps.

Brask barked out a laugh and smiled. "I thought she wasn't your concern?" The Igrakk Preyfinder was lazily reclining on the long white seat. "Hmm?"

The off-duty dark shirt and pants he wore were a lie. Stom eyed him sourly. If he hadn't grown to like the man, he'd have punched him, despite the audience behind them. Curse the Preyfinder system. None of them were ever truly off duty.

He never had a moment alone to contemplate what was happening…why he wanted so dearly to dive back in and slap some sense into Willow… He glared again at the screen, and at her, where she sat in her shorts, the sun gleaming off her long thighs. Slap her, then, in the dirty earth syntax, fuck her brains out.

"She's not my concern. But I gave her an out. If this woman would use it she'd survive for many years before this Aids takes her life."

What a waste that would be.

"I've been watching as you have. You know why she's not running. It's her friend, Ally."

She'd stopped burning her hand, had put away the device with the flame. Now, demons take everyone and chew on their bones, she was only crying quietly.

This earth woman was slowly killing him.

He sighed, sat back, and let the tension subside. "Yes. I know. She cares for her and this other one has problems adapting to new situations."

He absentmindedly traced the red spiral groove on his left bicep, remembering the first time he'd seen the matching one grow on Nasskia – a smaller, beautiful copy of his mark. Such wonderment had possessed him at the realization that he'd found his bond mate. Then he'd lost her and he'd vowed never to forget her, yet here he was lusting after this earth woman. Terrible.

What sort of person was he to so easily forget a vow?

"Even Feya sometimes take pets, Stom," Brask said gently.

"I never thought I was so shallow." He swallowed, unhappy at how he must look, sad, perplexed. The Preyfinder needn't know his every weakness.

For a second Brask lowered his head then he looked Stom in the eyes. "You're a Feya and a man. That's nothing to be ashamed of.

"Vows are not seeds blown in on the wind, they are rock."

"What did you avow?"

"Never to forget her." He inhaled, exhaled, thinking back to the time of her death and the destruction of Grearth. "Never to take another mate."

An Igrakk's hand descended on his shoulder and squeezed. Jadd, another of the big Preyfinders and one he knew had found a bond mate among the earth women.

He squatted beside Stom then gestured at the screen. "I know of your troubles but consider this. Sometimes we don't find our mates, they are given to us. I see much emotion in how you regard her."

"Emotion?" He shook his head, chuckling. "This is a hunt, not a women's meeting. And calling her my mate? You pervert the word. We are blessed with one true mate in our lives. One! I will not diminish that."

Perhaps he'd insulted Jadd. The man was trying to aid him. The two Preyfinders stared at him, saying nothing even though it made the silence ever more awkward as the seconds piled up.

He looked from one to the other. "You think I should go after her? Both of you think that?"

"I only give you a new fact to consider. It's up to you what you do." Jadd unfolded his legs and stood.

"Go after her?" Brask pulled an ugly face then gave Willow a long examination. "No. I think you should go fuck her."

"I see. I'm grateful for your astute advice, Brask."

"Of course you are." He grinned good-naturedly. "You know you want to."

"I do not want to go fuck her. I want to go drag her out of the danger area. I want to kill her enemies."

"And then?"

"Nothing. Leave."

But he stayed at the post watching her for many more hours, even as night descended, thinking, debating within himself. No one else was allowed to steer the drone, or to physically aid him in this surveillance. He had to sleep sometime. The nano-chem would have matured in her system by now. He could, theoretically, go out there, pretend to chase her, lose her, and leave this planet behind him, until naught was left of his memory of her except a scintillating warp trail disappearing into the black of space. His obligations would be done.

He could.

When it was one am, he parked the drone on the roof of her house, and shut it down. Then he turned onto his side on the thinly padded recliner, and forced himself to wind down.

She had a meeting tomorrow with this gun seller.

The truth was, he longed to do what Brask advised. He just didn't understand his desires. Why? Even while concentrating on battle he'd encountered many females, and he'd never desired any of them. Why Willow? Why did he also detest the thought of leaving her to her fate?

He set his internal wake-up to five am. When he closed his eyes, all he could see was her worried face as she chewed the nails on her pretty fingers. And the burning. He imagined himself cuddling her into his side and soothing her with touches and words. He smiled and the gentle tide of sleep washed over him.

The lightness of cloth registered on his skin. Someone had covered him with a blanket. A woman spoke, gently resting her hand on his arm. "You'll find your way, Feya. You will. You remind me of Jadd when he came to me. He and I will be one forever."

The saccharine advice dragged him up from dreamland and he popped open an eye then grunted. It was Jadd's bondmate, Brittany, a sweet woman. She made him think of gamboling mindless deer like in a film Brask had recently subjected him to. Bambi? That was it.

"Listen, Bambi. I appreciate your helpfulness but I need to sleep."

"Brittany." She smiled hesitantly.

"Go away. Please."

"Sorry. Of course. Sleep."

He awoke in a ruffled mood at five am, stripped his weaponry from the dummy awaiting him and strapped on his Heckler and Koch and the twin Magnums.

The drone routine was a standard warm-up, so he took the tablet to breakfast. With a triangle of toast in his mouth, he tapped buttons as they turned green. Toast and strawberry jam had taken some getting used to, the first times. Human food was different but tasty. He was careful not to get jam on the weapons.

Being armed at the breakfast table caused a few rude stares. He concentrated on the tablet.

"The Feya's got PMT," was all he heard Brask say. PMT? Whatever that was. The language app glitched at times. What did they all know about being a Hunter? Not that he was one. Or should be. Why was he doing this when he needed to leave this planet? The whole idea of chasing this alien female was anathema and the very opposite of what he should be doing.

He hadn't even said goodbye to Nasskia or seen her grave, or the graves of his children, and he never would. This was complete stupidity.

The last bite of toast a dry lump in his throat, he walked out to the surveillance room and flicked the switch. Screens flashed to life.

He sat to watch.

While cinching in the holster straps, he observed Willow sneak past the reservoir and through the trees for her meeting with the gun merchant. The little mellow green light on the life monitor on his chest strap flashed. His pulse was steady, blipping away. Good.

He was calm until the weapon, a Glock, was placed in her hand. Seeing her loading it and checking out the slider and the magazine, made something rumble to life inside him. When she tucked the gun into a bag, he hit some unexpected limit.

For a few moments, he pressed the center of his forehead with two fingers, circling, massaging away the tension. Instead of Nasskia when he woke up, his first thought had been of her, Willow. Was it just that she needed him?

That weapon in her hand had looked as out of place as a flower would in his. Killing was his occupation.

He stopped and stared at nothing, forearms leaning on his thighs. She did need him. So what if she was alien and there were a trillion more here also dying of one thing or another? This one, he could help.

This one had a sweet body that seemed to have been made to tempt him. His tongue remembered her taste, the feel of her nipple springing up as he sucked on her. The wetness between her legs, her groans and sighs…

"Dreaming, Feya?" Brask lightly punched his arm.

He grimaced. "Yes."

"Her?"

He dropped his head, clasped his hands. Why not say? "Yes."

"Look, if it's hurting you this much, just give her to me, I can get permission to take her off your hands. She can be my pet."

"What?" The idea of Brask touching her, running his hands over her. "Don't you dare –" He glared at Brask and found him smiling, with his hand out, and a red harness bunched up in his fist.

"You might need this with a spirited one like her. Collar, leash, gag. I can't take her from you, Stom. She's yours."

He eyed the thing – straps, dark red leather, bronzed buckles. Was this what Brask thought a pet should wear?

"I'm going down there now." He stood and stalked away, aware that between his eyes was ridged by anger, that he was glowering as he whipped his coat off the armor rack and over his shoulders. It settled in place, covering the machine pistol.

Brask was standing nearby, already in his coat, already armed.

"You're doing the second stage properly? Or is it a pretend one as you discussed with me days ago?" When Stom didn't reply, he added, "We need to know. We have to protect you, be ready to cover up for mistakes if humans become aware."

Pretend, or real? They wanted a blatant verbal declaration. He stood and his hand clenched on the width of the holster strap, squeezing it in. His pulse was blipping along a little faster, a little heavier. Determined to stay focused he opened his mouth to say the word, *pretend*. And baulked.

"Real. For now."

Bemused and appalled at himself, he shook his head. This had to be a betrayal of Nasskia. You couldn't squeeze out of vows with debates, tricky arguments, and special situations, could you?

The red harness had been left abandoned over a seat. The possibilities… He frowned. Other owners used such things on their pets.

"I wouldn't know what to do with that." But, on a whim, he picked it up and stuffed it into an inside pocket. "Let's go."

Chapter 8

There were things moving out there in the forest. Hiding a weapon in a bag when you were scared some gangster was about to knock you off seemed stupid. She searched blindly among the books she'd put in there for disguise, and pulled it out. The Glock felt right in her hand. Heavy. Like if you couldn't shoot them, you could at least hit them over the head with it. Though all guns made her think that.

Nicolai had moved off, disappeared, and left her to make her way back home. This was the edge of a small park that butted onto the messy wilderness around the reservoir.

The park itself was sometimes littered with needles and, well, litter. But once under the gum trees you saw less rubbish. The addicts liked to stay around the benches. Nicolai aimed for his meet-ups to be somewhere that CCTV was unlikely to see a handover. Between that and her desire to not go too far from the house…she'd picked here.

Willow looked around again. Another seventy yards and she'd be home. The noise had come from where Nicolai had gone.

The sun was up but slanting in at such an angle that the trees blocked most of the light. The crunching of leaves and small sounds she heard were distant, like maybe someone was struggling with someone else. Maybe Nicolai needed help? She hefted the gun, checked the safety was off and cautiously, trying not to make those leaf crackling noises, back tracked.

She made her muscles think. Care, take care. Move like a damn snake with feet.

Her sneaker-shod feet pressed on grass.

Crackle. Crunch.

Shit. She wasn't Pocahontas. How the hell did you stop leaves making noises?

Dark bars of trees. The glint of sun. Something flickered across her vision. She squinted, trying to make out whatever it was that moved there. It was big. If it was there at all. Then it vanished again.

Frantic, she scanned her surroundings. Left to right. Right to left. *Flick.* No. Nothing. *Flick.* What was that?

Someone screeched. The thing prowled in closer.

"Stay the fuck back." But fear had her throat and it had come out a whisper. Did she really want to yell and warn it…him? She raised the gun a tad from where it pointed groundward.

And closer. Squiggles of black and columns of tree bark gray shimmied across her eyes. She blinked. A man came at her.

The world shuddered, jellified, as a weird sort of joy rippled through her. Every muscle in her body cramped, her eyes rolled up for a flicker of time, and her hand clenched. The gun fired. Though she'd grabbed her wrist at the last second, the kick of the gun blew her hand back and up.

What the fuck?

Before she could figure out what had happened, he had her, hand jarring in around her neck, other on her wrist, flinging her back.

Her back thumped into tree. She coughed. The gun was ripped from her fingers.

"What were you doing?" he demanded.

She blinked into his face and recognized him by his scent before his voice or face registered. *Stom.* She inhaled again, aghast at her reaction, but wanting to wriggle like a puppy whose owner has arrived, or like a woman who has just the right man pinning her to a tree.

Fuck this. "You!" What was wrong with her?

As if the dawn had been waiting just to trick her, the light strengthened enough for her to see him clearly.

"Yes, me." His scowl wasn't going away.

"I'm sorry! I didn't know it was you. You scared the crap outta me!" Her thumping heart shook her. She was never *ever* going to say why she'd pulled the trigger, that she'd nearly had an orgasm.

"You didn't?" The words came out low and nasty enough to rivet her in place and set her to staring back at him.

"No. Obviously." Anger at him scaring her swamped her fear. "Dumbass."

Something wet dripped on her breast. In the light mottling her, ran a crimson rivulet of blood that tracked down into her cleavage, warm and terrifying.

"Is that blood?" Her stomach flip-flopped.

She looked at him. Dapples of leaf shadow and his dark markings flowed across his face. He was so difficult to see under the trees. Those eyes, those enchanting pale blue eyes, swiveled to look down at her breasts. His cheek dimpled as he twitched into a one second smile.

"Yes, it is. It's mine. You got my finger." His brow knitted as if he couldn't believe what she'd managed to do. "An armored coat on, never wounded in battle except once, and you manage to get me with this archaic earth weapon. Mark this, in my world an injury means you owe me something in return."

Armored coat? What the fuck? And she owed him? Sure she did.

Couldn't be too serious, if he was chastising her. "I didn't know it was you! Damn you, tell me you're coming next time…Mr. Alien. If that's what you are."

She tested his hold and despite his injured hand, it didn't give. "Let go, asshole. And give me back the Glock."

He ignored her, his eyes averted as if he listened to something.

When he spoke, it didn't make sense. "Yes, it is," he murmured. "No, it's not serious. If I have to, she's coming with me." On her throat, he lifted his fingers then repositioned them, playing with her neck, as if he'd found something fascinating. His gaze shifted again to her blood-smeared breasts.

Her nipples responded and went all perky, throbbing, and visible through her T-shirt.

Oops.

She needed a distraction. Fast. "There's something happening back there. I heard noises. My friend Nicolai –"

"Is being fucked by some woman. I don't think interfering is a good idea."

Fucked. The way he'd said it made it sound like a word for groveling around in the dirt while every imaginable perversion was done to you.

"How do you know that he's…doing that?"

His gaze was so intense, she wanted to squirm. She *did* squirm. Instincts. Shit. Her eyelids quivered down by a fraction as the front of her thighs met him down there. The coat was close. *He* was that close. Thank god he'd not unbuttoned it. Groin to groin, almost. Dangerous.

"Umm. You should move back, you know?"

"Oh?" As if he'd read her mind he switched hands, wrestled her wrists back to the tree when she made to break away, then began undoing buttons. The coat parted, button by button. Dazed at the sight, she watched. Very deliberately, he pushed his thigh between hers. When she noticed his smile it was grim, as if this were a chore he had to do.

Willow licked her lips, swallowed. "Back off and give me my gun."

"You think I'm going to let you, a woman who burns herself in her spare time for amusement, run around with a weapon?"

More buttons were undone. Another. And another. The bottom ones must have been free already. The coat swung wide.

"Burning? What?" Her mouth stayed open. How did he know she did that? He'd been spying? "You watched me!"

How had he seen her? She ran through possibilities. Telescope, but from where? Bugs. Alien weird surveillance thing. Funny how that seemed most likely. "How?"

"Yes, I watched you burn yourself. You're bad."

Bad was the last way she expected that to be described. Well it was, but, but…her thoughts petered down to nothing. All the cravings of the past day or so resurrected in a small tsunami. *Lust.* In front of her, was a man who embodied that in every molten move, in every cell of his well-sculpted body.

"I'm bad?" she whispered.

"You. Mmm." He lowered his head and scented her neck, lips pressing on her, here, there – kisses that stirred her more than they should, because they promised so much. Where else might he kiss? Drifts of air cooled her where his nose touched her skin, where he breathed on her.

"Bad. Definitely." Then he licked her neck, slowly, in one helluva long caress with his tongue, like a predator tasting his mate, before he kissed her softly again.

She shivered. *I don't know this guy. Not really. Am I such a slut?*

"You're beautiful. And you smell so good I want to eat you all up, every time I'm near. Why the fuck is that?"

The tinge of menace made her go up on her toes.

Then he bit the side of her neck, hard.

She keened, threatened by, enraptured by, the savagery of his teeth sinking into her muscle. Helpless, she shut her eyes. She tried not to let her collapsing legs make her slide down the tree trunk and straight to the ground. She had no wish to look like a weak female unable to resist…cause if she did, it seemed like he might take her, here, now.

His teeth let go.

Fucked against a tree. God. What an idea.

Where he held her wrists onto the bark, she tugged again, but even with a hurt hand his grip was fierce.

What had she done? She'd thought Stom the sort of man who needed an invitation to get going. Seemed as if shooting him had done the trick. Next time she wanted a date, she'd put a bullet in him.

He put his mouth to her ear, nuzzling her there, while he explored her below – fondling her breast, her belly, and her hip, then tugging up her T-shirt. He took a handful of her breast like he owned it, and squeezed so much it hurt.

Something about being forced against the tree, about him making her stay there while he played with her body, sizzled through her like lightning through rain.

If her throat hadn't closed in, if she didn't have to stick her tongue on the roof of her mouth to stop from groaning, she'd have said, no.

He drew back, grunted. "What is it about you? When I smell you, I have this compulsion to get more than close to you, I want to be inside you, to make the beast with two backs with you, to fuck you so hard and rough you'll find walking impossible."

Pinned mercilessly, she could only whimper. Words – gone.

Worse, what he felt was a mirror image of her.

"I don't want to do that. I don't want to *fuck* you. Feya don't fuck, we love. But for you, that human word…fuck. So right."

He bowed his head and kissed her furiously for a minute of lip-crushing mouth to mouth that was as passionate as sex, that left her panting and weak, and straining to free her hands so she could claw at him. When she craned forward to return the kiss, he nipped her lower lip then sucked on it. "Tell me, no?"

"I… Umm." No? Her mind and tongue had problems forming words. "I think… I think I need a dictionary to figure how to say that."

"Not surprising. I know why *you* desire me, Willow, but it shouldn't affect me. And it is."

One-handed, he shoved her shirt all the way up, ripped down her bra so both her breasts were free, then undid her belt, the button on her denim shorts, and the zip.

She did nothing but ache. He'd pinned her here because he wanted her right where she was.

Fuck.

"Not talking?" He raised a brow. "Is this attraction some secret woman thing we Feya don't have? What have you done to me?"

"Me?" She croaked out a word, shocking herself. "I can't *do* anything." He loosened her shorts some more. "Wait. Don't…" When she wriggled to elude him, that only that made her pussy move against his muscled thigh.

He pushed it into her more. Solid man. Solid thigh. Right there where it felt so *good*.

Her eyes rolled up.

"Don't? You should say no, fast." He had two fingers down the front of her panties, heading southward, cruising over her clit. "Faster than that, girl. Say something. Because. I really. Don't want. To do this."

"Liar," she croaked out, indignantly.

"Am I? I don't think so."

What?

Arm and body caging her, he watched her with those stone clear eyes, while his big hand tugged at her shorts and massaged her swollen clit. The denim shifted off her hips, exposing her panties. If he let her up, her shorts would likely fall to her ankles.

"Understand me?" Angry, so angry were those words of his.

"Yes." She gulped. Except she didn't. This was too sudden.

Despite his violence, she was responding. Involuntarily. The need growing. Whatever this exchange was, it wasn't love. Who cared? Not her. Not now. She closed her eyes, arched, moaned. Unfair. She couldn't help her reaction when he probed at her like that.

Breathing harshly through lips that seemed swollen, she opened them wider to speak. Try, try harder. This wasn't natural, wanting him so much. She *could* say it. "N –"

He came in and kissed her hard again, made the words go away, made her mind spin off into space.

"Take note. That kiss means I'm going to fuck you." Still pinning her onto the tree with his body weight, with his hand on her wrists and his leg between hers, he took something from his pocket, flipped it open, and swallowed the contents, then tucked it away.

He let her go.

The freedom was so unexpected it rocked her. The places he'd kissed and groped stung and hurt but most of all she was buzzing with the expectation of sex with this freaky god of a man.

Who she didn't know. Not really.

Am I a slut? Willow swayed, and went to cover her exposed breasts but he swept aside her arms.

He grabbed handfuls of her T-shirt beneath her armpits and stripped it off her, then dropped his coat and her shirt to the ground. Off balance, she was scared but so horny she was shaking. She reached to either push at him or pull him closer, she wasn't sure which, but he spun her around so she faced the tree, and shoved her into it.

"Stay." The growl from behind and above locked down her brain for seconds.

She had to stop this. Whatever compelled them both couldn't be good.

Fire. Imagine fire. The memory of pain cleared her head and freed her. Oh my. She'd popped her ass upward at him, presenting herself for easy access.

She straightened, turned. Crap. She shouldn't have looked.

Stom stood there, disheveled and wild-eyed, dark gray shirt sticking to his muscles. His zip was undone and his pants ready to be pushed down his legs. Casually, he pulled his shirt off over his head. Her mouth dried. The height difference and his crazy black-striped chest did even more to disturb her completely-not-normal perspective.

She ran her tongue across her lip, assessing him.

"Christ, you're hot. Man…"

Now was the time to say that no.

"Did I tell you to move?"

Unable to blink, in case she missed something, she stiffly shook her head.

"Good. I wanted an excuse." He bared his teeth. As if by magic, his hand held what looked a leash and collar. The other hand was bloody.

Feral had taken over.

The stripes on his face, neck, and chest stood out like warning signs, sheened with sweat.

She'd forgotten how strong a man could be, and Stom was more than a man.

Without warning, he spun her again, leaning on her to trap her against the coarse bark while he strapped the collar about her neck. She squeaked once then subsided and let him handle her as he wished to. This, this thing he did with the making her do things, the abruptness of him grabbing and taking, it blew her mind. Fuck equality. Fuck asking before he did it. With him, she wanted this – wildness, compulsion, animal ferocity.

Once on, the collar seemed to pulse at her neck. The thing circled her, ran tingles down into her body, calmed her even, as if it were more than plain leather. A haze settled in.

"Wait," she mumbled. "I never said I wanted this on."

"Quiet. This is not your want. It's mine." The leash clicked on and he secured it on a low branch. He slapped her ass. "Mine."

The reverberations of the slap echoed deep.

Mine. The word had a double meaning. His idea to leash her. His possession. She grew wetter in an instant.

Rough yet businesslike, he kneeled and pulled her shorts all the way down her legs until they bunched above her sneakers. He was going to fuck her after all.

Any normal woman would stop him.

And yet she moved not at all. Maybe she wasn't normal.

His naked hands clasped her hips. Skin contact. Things were about to happen. He was going to put his cock in her. Damn. She sucked in air.

"Arch your back. Let me see your pussy."

He wanted her to stick her butt out. She'd not had sex for a year. But Stom...damn. Slowly, she did as he'd asked and even tried to part her thighs, despite the shorts constricting her ankles.

He stepped back, admiring her. "That's good. Pink. Pretty. I like the color." Then his voice growled deeper. "Though red, my red, would be far better. If you were marked with my color..." Gently, almost reverently, he touched her down there, then with his other hand he angled her outward and made her push her ass higher.

From the slick and smooth way his finger travelled along her cleft, she was very wet. She heard the intake of his breath. He liked her like this. Moist for him. The pleasure of that warmed her.

"This is your cunt, Willow? It's my cunt now. Hear that?" As he spoke, he slowly circled the inner edge of her pussy with one finger, teasing her with desire.

Fuck. She quivered. His dirty talk hit every *take me* button inside her head. She held back for only a fraction of a second before she nodded. Wiggling her butt seemed an excellent idea, and she pushed back onto his fingers. When he resisted impaling her, she whined and bit her lip.

Lip still caught in her teeth, she lowered her forehead to the bark. The sound of his pants being pulled off warned her. She shifted her legs even farther apart, sure he must be looking at her there. Her entrance clenched. Ugh. Slow man. If she didn't get him inside her, she'd implode from lust overload, and how would that look on her death certificate?

Then his cock breached her and shoved apart the entrance to her pussy. He speared inside her: that exquisite instant of impalement, fullness. She forgot everything but that, mesmerized by the building rhythm of sex. Stom was taking her, inside her, his body slapping against her ass. *Yes.*

He must have loosened the leash. His hand was behind her nape gathering it in his fist.

"Look at me." He turned her to face him and touched foreheads, with his hand wedged around her chin. Between collar, leash, hand, and his cock pumping at her, he totally controlled her. She couldn't move a fraction, open her mouth, or tongue her lip, without him seeing her arousal. He observed her every pant and whimper, kissing her mouth while he fucked her.

"Look at me," he whispered. "Look at me."

And she did – she opened her eyes wider. Captured. Bound in the storm of his need. Her air was his. *She* was his.

He inched her up the tree until her toes barely touched earth. The slow rhythm of his thrusts strengthened – faster, harder, deeper inside, making her dig fingernails into the bark. He engulfed her in passion. Her thighs shook. Ecstasy was but a moment, a cry, a helpless whimper away.

Flattened into the tree by his most powerful thrust, her clit rocked against the bark. He kissed her over her mouth, feeding on her lust, and rammed in one last time, gasping as his seed swelled into her.

For what seemed ages he stayed there, over her, his thick muscled arms barring her from stirring. Then he woke from the lethargy of post-orgasm and bit her neck and shoulders in several places, no doubt leaving the deep arcs of his teeth. And bruises. Those too.

But she hadn't come. Lovers should make her come. Wasn't it her right?

Legs trembling, she slurred out the statement, and he laughed.

"You think so? No, Willow. You may make me want to ravish you and fuck you every possible way when I see you but before I will let you come, you'll pay homage to my cock."

"I'll what?" She frowned. This wasn't in the handbook.

*****

Mandy stood over the man, smiling. The injection had taken him quickly and he lay unconscious, his head flopped to the side. The factory queen would like this one. He had an intriguing scent about him. Weapon scent. Drugs scent. A criminal, the data had suggested. This was her best convert yet.

She took his ankle and began to drag him through the undergrowth toward her car. Whatever associates he had, she would find them and convert them too.

When the nerve chewers eat their way to this one's brain and make him one of us, I will begin on his friends.

Maybe they would know some witches.

Chapter 9

"You're coming back with me," Stom repeated. Where had that homage to his cock idea come from? It had spewed out of his mouth. When she'd looked horrified – he'd felt an amused yet mean sort of triumph. Odd. Not him.

"No, I can't. Nope."

"Really?"

She defied him, but a trickle of sweat ran down her face, she still struggled to catch her breath, and she was using the tree to hold herself up. Sexual devastation. His balls tightened.

He grunted.

Her dumbfounded look meant nothing to him. There wasn't time to explain. Taking her here had been foolish. He'd spilt blood everywhere. Alien blood to these earth people. If a laboratory got a sample that would mean a big clean up. Semen was just as bad as blood but harder to see and keep intact.

The Preyfinders would clean up the blood and the cum.

He couldn't leave her because she was going to die if he left her alone. Buying a gun wasn't going to save her but leaving her here might kill her.

And there was the other reason – that he couldn't bear to let her go.

He hated that, and when she'd asked if he was going to let her climax, and he'd said no, he hated that too. His cruel rejection had been a perverse way to defeat his first instinct – to care for her needs. Not understanding why he'd wanted to do that had made him mean. And he'd ended up less caring than any man should ever be of his lover.

But he didn't like being dictated to, not even when it was by his own body.

He shouldn't take this out on her. She was just a woman. Or was she? Something here was deeply flawed, deeply wrong.

When she pulled up and buttoned her shorts, despite the mess he'd left on her thighs, he watched everything. He was fascinated, adoring, and pissed off. Her scowl after he'd told her he wasn't letting her come, had made him want to do more nasty things to her. Everything here seemed wrong, in so very many ways.

He wanted to pull her shorts down again and play with her, to bend her over his lap and stare at the damage – at his cum dribbling from her pussy. This puzzled him so much he was going to wear a track in his brain from thinking it over and over.

"Come get us," he said quietly to his watchers.

"I can't leave with you, Stom. I have Ally to look after. I'm not –"

He dragged her to him, whipped the leash around her wrists, and when she began to yell, he thanked Brask for his forethought, for once, and stuck the breath-through black gag in her mouth.

"Thirty seconds. ETA," someone called in his ear comm.

They'd been observing, of course. He wondered if any of them got their kicks from watching him plundering Earth pussy. Probably. Who wouldn't when it was a female as cute as… Why? Why was she so attractive to him?

He examined her, trussed, gagged, quiet for once, shifting from foot to foot as if thinking about running. He'd catch her in seconds and she knew it. Though he'd pulled her T-shirt down to cover her, it bunched oddly about her breasts. Sweat stuck those sweet black curls to her forehead and those pretty brown eyes blinked at him ferociously.

He sighed. He had no idea. She was just gorgeous. Even if she had almost shot his finger off.

He picked up everything and dressed quickly. Ignoring her squeals, he hoisted her onto his shoulder, and carried her to the forest edge so he could rendezvous with the black car in which the Preyfinders arrived. Quiet street. No one was observing them. Two Preyfinders he didn't know got out and one whipped open the passenger door. They nodded. He nodded, made Willow get in the back, then slid in after.

One of them, the front passenger, turned and threw back a question while he checked out the tied and gagged Willow. "Nice morning?"

"Yes."

She wavered from blatant terror to anger and she grumbled through the gag. Her eyes seemed ready to shoot bolts of lightning.

Which he ignored. "Shh. They're safe." He patted her thigh.

"Get what you wanted?" The man's eyes said he meant Willow.

His voice deepened into don't-you-even-think-of-approaching-her territory. "Yes."

"Good. We can't touch her. Not in the rules. You know that." He turned away.

Yeah, he did. It didn't hurt to make sure.

The car surged forward.

His finger was still oozing blood, all over the upholstery. Willow had some smeared on the curve of her breasts where they pushed out above her neckline. He leaned in and looked at those breasts, then took her face in his hand even though she dodged.

Her small defiance was both amusing and good to see. What a little fire cat he'd caught.

"Remember, you owe me for this." He held the finger with the piece missing from it up to her nose. "Cock homage."

She grunted meanly. More lightning bolts.

That made him smile and he settled beside her, watching the streets whizz past. What a morning.

Back at the canal house that overlooked the lake, he waited for the garage door to lower before getting Willow out of the car.

The others let him do it, not raising a hand to help. Of course. As he strode up the hallway, he patted her behind where he'd shouldered her. She was his to deal with. Rules of the game. They'd rescued him so he could get medical treatment. Willow was his to rescue though. Or to discard.

On his trip through the house, she grew quieter and less wriggly, perhaps looking at this dwelling. It was luxurious, by human standards, with its cool colors, grandiose ceilings and floor-to-ceiling frost-stippled glass looking out over the lake. No one could see in, of course.

He needed to get over to the Preyfinder ship that hid under the waters of the lake, but he wasn't allowed to take Willow across there. Not unless he made her truly his.

That wasn't happening. He needed no pet. This was temporary.

When he opened the secret panel to reveal the stairs leading down, she resumed squeaking and struggling. No matter, he held her still until he reached the capture room. He toppled her onto the big square bed that was set in the middle of the floor space. She decorated the ivory and azure blue quilt rather well. All those long, shapely limbs...

Stom sighed and took off the gag.

For a few seconds she only swallowed and ran her tongue around the inside of the mouth. "What are you doing? With me?" Willow looked around, her tone cautious. "You know you can't do this. This is illegal, immoral, you can't keep me here. I have to get back to Ally. She can't survive without me."

Can't? Did she not value his presence? Wait. He hardened his mind. What did this matter to him? She was but a temporary mate. An easy lay as the humans called it.

Only that term seemed insulting. She was too...too something he couldn't define for him to want to insult her.

"I respect you for your devotion to your friend, but she can survive a day without you. We will watch your house."

Her bosom heaved as if she tried to control herself but couldn't.

"Am I scaring you, Willow?"

She merely blinked then ventured, "A little. What are you?"

"I am what I said I am. An alien. I only brought you here because I'm worried you're going to get yourself killed."

"I so believe that."

Sarcasm again? He guessed what he'd just done to her in the forest made a mockery of what he'd said.

"It's true."

"Yeah? You and your two *friends* should look at yourselves in the mirror." The words snagged a few times as she said them.

"They're Preyfinders, merely doing their jobs. You heard what they said – they won't touch you."

Him, on the other hand.

He leaned over her, careful not to drip blood on the quilt, tipped her on her side, and undid the binding he'd made with the leash. Her small fingers tempted him to kiss them, and so he did. Then he straightened again, determined to be more aloof despite the way her body lured him, despite his cock being uncomfortably hard. Had he not fucked her fifteen minutes ago?

"Don't be scared. I saved you once."

"I bet most serial killers use that line." She squirmed into a seated position, propping herself up with straight arms. "So, you brought me here just to discuss philosophy."

Her toes scrunched in. Her mouth was straight. He couldn't miss those details on her. He seemed to absorb every movement she did.

Philosophy? It took him a moment to recognize the meaning. Then he took a hold of her chin with finger and thumb. "No. Not that."

When she glanced down at his groin, he narrowed his eyes.

"I'm not a whore, Stom. I couldn't help myself back there. You gave me something."

Even if it made no sense, her words stirred anger in him.

"And what did you give me? What I feel is not natural either."

That stopped her. "You said that before." She shook her head, eyes blazing, teeth showing as she spoke. "I did *nothing* to you. All I know is that you made me stand still for you to fuck me in public and I didn't stop you. Damn. That's sick. Oh shit. No protection! How the fuck did I forget that?" She screwed up her face into all sorts of horrified looks then buried it in her hands. Her next question was muffled. "Am I going to get pregnant?"

"No. You can't."

"Why? This better be good."

"Because I'm an alien."

"Bad answer, man." She stared wildly around the room and at the leash, then plucked at the collar. "I don't know what to believe anymore. I've been abducted and tied up and I've seen zero spaceships."

"You need to believe me." His finger was hurting badly but he tried to think. What could he show her? He wasn't allowed alien artifacts or to take her to the ship.

"Go away. Please?"

She flopped over onto her stomach. He heard her sniff and wondered if she cried. The females did that easily here. This did not make sense. Nothing about his reaction did. He'd get checked for foreign substances and invading infections while his finger was fixed.

Gods. The length of her stretched out on the bed, the inviting curves of her posterior where the shorts molded inward, the hint of wetness on her thighs. Her *smell* – his and hers mixed with the smell of recent sex. He ran a hand through his hair and shook his head.

"Find some clothes to wear. There will be women's clothing over there on the table." The neatly folded, squared-off piles on the elegant table by the far wall should have various dresses. Though he was sure she'd prefer shorts and T-shirt. "Don't remove the collar or I will do something bad to you when I return."

Her growl was cute.

"Do not test me."

If he waited much more he'd do something bad to her *now*, especially when she squeezed her thighs together as if pressing her pussy onto the bed.

Fuck.

He turned, stepped outside then closed and locked the steel door. He slumped, leaning his shoulders against the wall before thumping his head back. She gave him filthy ideas every second he was in her presence. Tests! He needed those. He probably had some deadly earth disease.

He went to walk away but something made him silently unlock and open the door again, just to see, whatever, maybe to see if she'd moved.

She hadn't. From the noises, she was crying. An unfamiliar sting started in his eyes and he had to resist the *pull* inside that demanded he go to her and hug her to him. Sad. She was so pretty, so small, so in need of a protector. He shut the door quietly, and held the handle tight enough to make his hand white and red from blood flow problems. What was *wrong* with him?

The two Preyfinders agreed to rig up a surveillance drone to use from the house. They couldn't help him catch or tend to Willow but Ally was separate. Not his. Not anyone's. If they needed an excuse for their next report, they could say it was an assessment of her qualifications as future prey. Hah. But this way he kept his promise to Willow.

The march along the white corridor to the ship airlock gave him time to think, to sort priorities. The quicker he did all this, the quicker he could return to her.

Fix finger and do tests. Then go back and, what was it Brask said? Fuck her brains out while he figured out what to do. He didn't want her getting killed out there. She wasn't moving without Ally. And he needed to fuck her even if he had no idea why.

Even now he recalled the feel of her pussy around him as he entered her. His mind followed the prompt of that memory. His cock sliding in. Her cunt all wet and hot. Exquisite. Him, claiming her for the first time, biting her neck. Teeth on her, the salty taste of her sweaty female skin. Her small cries. He swallowed.

"Wonderful," he muttered. At least Nasskia would never know he'd betrayed her. Alas, that didn't soothe his heart or his soul. Taking this Earth woman was wrong. Anger simmered.

There was a possible cause he hadn't considered. How devious was Brask?

The medical bay was empty of all bar the medic and him to start with, but while the medic put a regenerative splint on his finger, he called Brask.

The Preyfinder strolled in looking professional yet relaxed in black pants and shirt, his hair spiked up in sand-gold pieces and his face grim.

"What you got there, Stom?" He peered at the see-through splint. The thing was still connected by a lead to the cyber doc. Brask whistled. "Your pet took a good chunk of that finger off. Bone missing?"

Stom let him do his assessment. Besides, it felt like the machine was sucking the very flesh off his hand. He kept his teeth clamped as it hummed through another healing cycle.

The medic replied tersely. "Only the top joint. Minimal blood loss due to Stom's combat profile. It'll be about a week and a half before the finger is normal."

Brask looked up and met Stom's eyes. "I hope it hurts. You were careless. Walking into that."

True. "I've had worse. I'll survive. Now. Tell me what you gave me."

"Me? I gave you nothing. What do you mean?"

"Why am I so attracted to this Earth woman?"

"You are?" Brask smiled. He went back a step and perched on a stool. "I guessed it. I don't know why you are, let's say, attracted. Not my doing. Go with the flow. Take her as your pet. Simple answer."

Nothing? "Not your doing? You didn't give me anything? No chems?"

"No. On my soldier brother's honor."

"Ah." He blinked. That had been his best chance. An Earth disease had seemed very unlikely. "It must be some bug I picked up here then?"

The medic tapped the display on a screen near his elbow, "No. You've nothing wrong with you except for being a Feya with fingers that get in the way of bullets."

Stom leaned in and peered. "That was fast. You're sure?"

"Am I sure?" The medic frowned then unplugged the lead to Stom's finger splint. "No, I'm not. Look! I was wrong. You do have a disease."

The tone was so exaggerated he was wary. "What is it?"

The reply was matter of fact as the medic rose, packed away cables, and turned off equipment. "A virulent strain of purple *kak* disease and your dick's going to drop off tomorrow."

Brask guffawed. "Well saved, Yakul."

The man nodded to them both, saluted, and moved away.

"Ha ha. Not funny."

"I'm not sure why you have to question it, Stom. Be happy. My men tell me you have her locked in at the house. Go to her. You can keep her there for a day before you have to release her. Then it's one more capture. One dose of the nano-chem and that's it. Take her home with you."

Home. "I have no home. I have *no* use for a pet." Why didn't he understand that?

"Feya honor? I don't get that. This is sex. You deserve some fun in your life. No one can live without fun. You *are* an honorable man. This changes that not at all."

The man was trying to make him feel good about this situation. "Thank you." He hauled himself upright. "I'll think about it."

He would. That was true, but he also knew his honor was his own to regulate. He was the only one who could decide what was right.

A tap at the entrance to the hospital facility, at the far end of the room, made him turn. "Bambi," he muttered under his breath.

"What?" Brask looked also. "Brittany? Come in!" He gestured to her as he spoke in an aside to Stom. "She's fine, Stom. Just a quiet sort. She likes to check on anyone who's ill."

A sparrow flew into the room and landed on her shoulder. Strange.

He watched her stride lithely toward them, curious to see if he felt any of the same extreme attraction to her as he did to Willow. Her mane of glossy auburn hair flicked across her shoulders. Her hips swayed under the close fitting white uni-suit. But she meant nothing to him despite her beauty. Pretty, yes, but no more than that.

Whereas Willow, even now he felt the lure. He imagined her still crying and for once the need to comfort her dragged at him more than the need to have sex. Good. That was something any normal and good man would feel. Though perhaps not Brask – the Igrakk had a casual regard for women.

"You let her do this? See all the injured? Without questioning her why she wants to?"

"Yes, I do. I have a theory about the healing rates here. Just haven't quite figured it out yet."

He gave Brask a sharp glance before greeting Brittany. When asked, he let her examine the splint and even smiled and thanked her. With Brask's clue he was especially alert.

When she left, he stared into the splint. There seemed a subtle change.

"Wish it had still been connected to the lead. Yakul might've been able to get some data."

"You think she heals people?" Stom flexed his finger. It certainly stung less.

"I do. I'd discuss it further with Dassenze but he's gone off-planet. Small escalation of the war. There's a Bak-lal accumulation of war ships in a nearby system." He shot Stom a serious look. "Dassenze has an on-running investigation of some of the earth women. Odd things have been happening. Spikes in data."

"Does Brittany's bond mate, Jadd, know of this?"

"Not yet. Though I think he suspects." He sat forward, face still as stone, staring at the floor a moment. "If this is correct, it's the stuff of myths. No other starfaring race can do anything like this."

They regarded each other. Momentous, if true. Why had he not already told Dassenze? Obviously, he wanted more proof. Besides, the god was already aware of the possibilities.

Dassenze was the current Ascend god assigned here. If *he'd* left to assist in the war, what was he doing fooling around with capturing a woman? Stom drummed his fingers on the counter top beside him. He grimaced at the lance of pain. Wrong hand.

"Perhaps that's why I'm drawn to Willow. I knew there was something."

"A weird power?" Brask grinned. "Maybe. Maybe, you have a succubus on your hands. Lucky Feya."

"A suck you what?"

His grin widened. "That's a type of mythical Earth creature that lures men to have sex with them. Stom, if you do continue with this, I should tell you we may be short of Preyfinders for a while. We're gearing up to raid a possible focus of Bak-lal soldiers in the USA. We have to be doubly cautious without a god here to oversee. You're lower priority. So be careful."

"I thought this planet was clear? That you destroyed the only known factory queen?"

"We thought so. But it's possible there are more. Deep-buried ones. We can handle it. Last time we used the ship." He knocked on the arm of his chair. "*Doomslagger* did her job well, but I doubt we'll need her."

Taking out a queen would need ship firepower. He relaxed a little. They must only expect some stray soldiers.

He stood. "I'm going back to her. I'll keep mindful of what you said. But I am me. I march to my own brand of honor."

Brask twisted his mouth then grunted. "You do what you feel is right."

As he walked back along the underwater tunnel, a thought occurred to him. If Brittany could heal soldiers, she was a valuable prize. Lucky for him that Willow might only be a – what had Brask called her? A succubus. An enticer of men. Lucky because no one was likely to command him to make her his pet. Of course, Brask had been joking, but he didn't know what this desire for her felt like. Powerful enough that he had a hard-on whenever he even vaguely thought of going to her. Like now. He adjusted his cock and sighed.

Not since he was a youngling had he been so constantly aroused.

But, wait, if she *did* have any odd powers they'd still want her to see how she did it. Even if it was a useless power. Which meant if he didn't capture her, someone else might be ordered to. Anger crackled through his bones. He crushed his fists into tight balls.

Wait. Wait…

He pressed his fingers to his head. There was a flaw in his idea. No one else felt like this around her. His argument was kak. Something must be happening. But not that. Scratch succubus off the list.

When he resumed walking, a sense of dread occupied him. Not understanding this was unraveling his sense of self. He didn't know who he was anymore, except that he wasn't the pristine hero Nasskia and his younglings had clung to when he returned home from battle, not anymore.

He wanted her, he didn't want her. He wanted to keep his honor intact as well as her. Most of all, he wanted to stay true to his first love.

With barely twenty yards to go, he received the first automated warning. The room was on fire. And she was inside.

He sprinted.

He tore through the lock sequence in seconds, ripped open the door, and beheld a large inferno in the middle and bonfires reaching toward the ceiling elsewhere. The bed was on fire. At the opening of the door, a torrent of smoke poured past him, blinding him, choking him. As he strode forward, he was already barking out a command to the Preyfinders to manually activate the fire suppression systems, and in between that, he was screaming her name.

Why weren't the Preyfinders here? If this was rules again, he might kill them both.

Was she dead? Hurt? Lying somewhere among this fire writhing from burns?

"Willow! Willow, where are you!" He spun, tears streaming down his face from the terror that possessed him as well as from the smoke. If she were dead… An arm raised from the shadows and fire to the left then seemed to twist in an unnatural way. Stom leapt over and threaded past burning debris, racing to get to her. Was she on the floor?

But she wasn't there. Or had he missed the place? Was she here? He spun, searching through the pall of smoke, but couldn't see her. "Willow! Answer me." He kicked and tore flaming clothes from the blazing piles, making sure she was not beneath them. Then he spun around in another circle, searching with his eyes, though they stung. "Willowww!"

The smallest sound drew him to look behind him, and above the roar and crackle of flame, he heard footsteps.

Suppressant foam hit the room as he ran out and he passed the two Preyfinders as he dashed up the stairs.

"Seen her?" he yelled.

They kept going but one jabbed backward over his shoulder.

When they'd opened the secret door, she must've dashed out. They'd not stopped her. Fucking Preyfinder rules.

He caught her in the corridor, tackled her, then threw her over his shoulder and left the house and burning room to the others. The subtle whine of an engine and lack of smoke out here said they had some way of concealing the fire. The Preyfinders had easily controlled it, yet without his intervention, they'd have let her burn.

Terrifying. It hammered home the fact that she was his and no other's: his to throw away, to let die, or to guard from all the dangers of the universe. He could be her world, if he so desired. She could be his world, if he'd let her in. Complicated, so complicated. Where was the thousand page *Guide to Your Heart and Soul* when he needed it?

"Stom," she demanded in a wobbly voice. "Let me down."

He smacked her on the butt once and kept walking. Apart from a weak couple of kicks, she gave in.

Outside, beneath the trees at the edge of the lake, he waded into the water with her in his arms, letting the cold water soothe the burns on his hand. Weeping willows and the angle of this tiny cove shielded them from onlookers.

Though he hadn't restrained her, to his shock, she made no further attempt to escape. Instead she slipped to her feet when he let her down then stood shaking from head to foot. She didn't meet his eyes.

He watched her grimly as he dipped his hands in the fluid coolness. The water trickled musically.

"Do you have a death wish?"

Her shoulders slumped. Then she gave one wrenching sob and took his blistered hand at the wrist. At least it was the same one she'd shot. There were fresh tears on her begrimed face and more ran down through the soot as she gently turned his hand.

"I'm sorry." She sniffed. "You're hurt…I never meant to get you hurt. I'm so sorry." Her sobs wrenched at his heart and he raised her chin with his other hand and caressed her cheek with his thumb.

Then, wordless, he pulled her to his chest and sat in the sandy mud at the edge of the water, among the reeds and water lilies, with her clutched to him. He bowed his head and kissed her hair.

"It's okay. I'm not hurt badly. Small burns. It's nothing. Can you breathe okay?"

She nodded.

As she kept crying, he could feel the shakes of her body but gradually she calmed.

She might have meant to escape but he didn't care at all about that, not in the face of her misery over his pain. He'd been ready to explode with grief at the thought she might have died back there. And she – he took in a long, aching breath – she felt something the same. This was crazy.

He patted her, the water lapping at his knees where they stuck above the lake's water. "What are we going to do, Willow?" he whispered.

But she only shook her head a little, laughed in a wretched way, and snuggled in closer.

Chapter 10

She hadn't meant to hurt him, but she had. And if he'd not returned in time, she would have died in the room.

"I thought someone would come to get me out before it got that bad," she said to him, not courageous enough to look him in the eyes. He'd yell at her now, but he didn't.

"I'm sorry they didn't, but you're safe. I've got you now." Then he did make her look at him. The sadness in those blue eyes made her bite her trembling lip. "Promise me you won't do that again."

Why should she promise that? But before she could think it through some more, she nodded. Then she felt underwater in her shorts pockets, and pulled out the lighter. When she put it on his palm, he smiled and tsked at her.

The gentle forgiveness in his words and actions made her smile back. Was her mind going? All she wanted to do was please him and keep him safe. The tears kept dripping down her face. She sniffled and wiped them away, feeling stupid. When he only hugged her more, the trickle of tears turned into a constant flow and ragged sobs choked from her.

At last he struggled to his feet with her in his arms. "Come. You need something more than this. I don't want you to say anything. Just let me…" With her head laid against his chest, she could hear him swallow. "Let me take care of you."

The words, *I'm not a child*, came to her but remained unsaid. As her personal colossus walked up the steps and through the garden to the house with her cradled in his arms, she kept her eyes open and yet she wondered if she'd truly died and gone to heaven.

Let me take care of you. For as long as she could recall, no one had ever said those words to her.

She clutched at his shirt, wrinkling her forehead as that thought sank in deep, and something inside her broke.

Chapter 11

There was a shower upstairs next to the big bedroom so he carried her up there, wanting to wash away the smoke smell and still overcome by this grating, incessant need to make her whole again. That she'd almost killed herself trying to get away from here, from him, seemed the worst condemnation ever.

Under his feet were pretty rugs and a polished timber floor. He left footprints of soot and lake water on everything he walked over. The shower was big enough for a small war. The walls and floor were made of some pale stone and the shower bits and pieces were shiny and looked like poetry in metal. He didn't pay any of this much heed for the woman in his arms meant so much more.

When she tried to speak he shushed her. He removed the collar from her neck, despite a momentary regret. It looked so right on her. Then he set to work undressing her, pulling off her wet T-shirt and shorts, kneeling to ease down her panties, getting her to step out of them, undoing her bra. He told his rude cock to stay out of it despite the unrelenting sexual reminders as he handled her pliant female body.

With her undressed, he swallowed, held his breath, and turned away to adjust the faucets. Then he urged her under the flow of water, found the soap and stopped dead, mouth dry. Nipples, breasts, and when he looked lower, the gorgeous way her legs met and her sex peeked out in that pretty divide...and his cock was so upright he'd snap it off if he tried to get it down.

"Hmm?" Wide-eyed, she looked as dumbstruck as him. "We can't do this."

No. He cleared his throat and backed her further under the shower then began soaping her.

Amazing how he managed, even getting her to turn around so he could wash her hair and watching the water flow in rippling and twisting currents down her back. Her muscles were heaven under his hands. Smoothing away the residues of soot on her pleased him immensely. It hit some spot inside him that made him know, yes, he was doing good.

Her soft noises of pleasure made him have to stop once or twice to reassemble his brain, but he kept going. Clean her. Get her right.

Make her a woman again and not some soot-covered succubus.

Suck. The word in his mind made his cock twitch and his fingers dug into her shoulders.

"Ow!" Willow flinched and spun around, almost slipping on the wet stone.

Her full breasts jiggled, swayed. The pink-brown centers drew him. They were all puckered up from the play of water over them, or perhaps from his rushed soaping. The two little taut buds had been under his palms, bubbles of soap catching on them...

"Oh," she murmured, looking down at where his pants were pushed out by his erection.

When she didn't raise her eyes and the very tip of her tongue emerged from her lips to curl moistly against them, he groaned.

This wasn't why he'd kept her, remember? He needed to sort out her life, somehow. Stop her getting killed. Sex was just, was not... He inhaled a shuddery breath.

She twisted her mouth and took a partial step toward him, enough that she nudged his pants and, more importantly, pushed into the tip of his cock with her stomach. Her mischievous smile as she rolled her hips side to side, pushing at him some more, made him growl.

"Stop." He took her shoulders, all too aware of what parts of her he could take hold of if he slipped his hands lower. "It's midday and I want to get you fed. I doubt you've eaten today. Have you?"

As if pretending innocence, she shook her head, but moved into his cock. He *had* told her she should pay homage to his cock. Tempting, so tempting.

"Demanding little thing. Aren't you hungry? For food?" He cradled her chin in his palms and toyed with her mouth until she opened and took one of his thumbs inside. The wet suction went straight to his groin. This time he shut his eyes, sure he'd come from her doing this alone if she kept it up.

"Mmm." Her little female tongue licked all up and down the tip and she sucked audibly.

A pulse of heat ran up through his cock. Cornering her against the wall, getting her to open her legs, and shoving into her became his number one priority.

But when he felt her let go, he snapped open his eyes, and grabbed her arms.

"Come." He steered her out of the shower, dripping, sexy, and ready for him. When he only threw a towel over her and began to dry her hair, she grumbled. "No, Willow. You need to eat."

The things he made himself do, but he had this weird longing to do this at his speed, when he wanted to, and not when she demanded it. He ignored his steel-hard member and toweled her dry. Whatever need for sex raged within him clearly also consumed her, but he loved doing this his way, so much so that he began to tease her with his fingers beneath the towel – pushing the cloth into her cleft, rubbing the mounds of her breasts. When she was squirming into his touch, he put a lock on her neck from behind so she couldn't move, and he slipped his hand down over her ass. He splayed his fingers to appreciate the shape of that delicious globe then pushed his whole hand between her legs.

Slick. Wet. Plump lips.

"This isn't water down here. It's you. Want something, girl?"

He laughed when she wriggled on his hand then again at her shocked stillness as he found the right spot, nudged his finger in, and ever, so, gradually, curved the tip of that finger up inside her. He left it there for a while, exploring no more than an inch of her but making circles and tugging at her lips, doing tiny thrusts, and widening her.

Soon her sobbing moans demanded he did more but he held back.

When he had her sopping wet, arching her spine backward to where he penetrated her, and panting, he murmured in her ear, "I think that's enough." He let her go. She staggered and seemed mesmerized.

Whatever chaotic thought had brought her to set fire to the room, she'd recovered. He made a decision then and there. They needed to talk. But after. After what? Feeding her? Sex? This animalistic attraction was screaming at him. And having her staring at him, wet lipped, glazed of eye, with her pussy so obviously swollen and ready for him that his toes curled looking at her, *this* was tangling up his brain.

He didn't want a pet, but he couldn't stop himself, not now, not when he had her like this. *Traitor*, whispered deep in his head. He wavered. Later, afterward, talk. Not *now*.

"Wait." He stripped off his wet clothes, his shirt, pants, and underwear. Experimenting, pleased at how she avidly watched him, he ran his hand up and down his cock. She watched that too.

When she went to say something, he added, "Don't speak."

He wondered how much this lust within her would let him go. Willow hadn't seemed a woman to obey if she had other notions. "If you speak, I promise you, I will tease you all day and all night with my tongue on you down there, and I won't let you orgasm." He flicked his finger at the door. "You first. To the kitchen downstairs."

She huffed out a big exasperated sigh, while eyeing his erection, but then she turned and headed out the door.

The exaggerated wiggle of that ass had to be deliberate and he found himself not breathing. She taunted him. This was a fascinating game.

With both of them naked, collecting everything from the kitchen was a painful test in how to ignore a nude woman. She helped him gather a bowl of fruit, fresh bread and cheese, and they took it all to the dining table.

"Stand there." He pointed to the floor in front of a chair then sat in it. His cock bobbed enough to attract her gaze. "I'm going to feed you and I'm going to play with you. If you make a sound, I get to bite you somewhere."

He didn't say why – that he was doing it this way because he couldn't bear to keep his hands off her any longer. His eyes were probably twinkling with evilness. He sure felt evil. Damn, this was fun. If they didn't fuck soon, they might both explode.

Interest flared in her eyes.

Still holding her gaze, he reached out and trailed his finger from her belly button downward, meandering a little when it reached the softness of her mons, circling, but then he found her clitoris. The little thing had popped out where he could easily find it. Like him, she seemed in a permanent state of arousal.

"I pray…" He toggled her clit from side to side, tracing around it and over it, amused at how she'd shivered. "I pray you make lots of noises."

Her eyelids fluttered to half-mast and she sighed as he kept toying with her. When he explored further, his digit easily slid between her legs into her moisture.

"I hope you don't mind your own taste on your food."

Then he stopped, reached across to the bowl, and selected an apricot. She pulled a disgusted face and made a small unhappy squeak.

"That's what I like to hear."

Before she could figure out why, he drew her to him, her feet shuffling, and he nipped her belly. When she squealed, he did it again. His teeth marks showed white, then red.

"Mmm." He kissed the indentations on her skin then offered her the fruit. "Yours."

She nibbled cautiously on the apricot with her front teeth, chewing a tiny bite.

"All of it." Without finesse, he stuffed the rest in while he trapped her in place with his hand at the small of her back. When she swallowed, he grinned.

For a while he simply fed her cheese, bread, fruit, and sips of water.

"Sit." He patted one thigh and waited for her to gingerly settle.

Their kissing began languorously. They found a rhythm, discovering each other with their lips and tongues, playing coy and playing aggressor. Finally he grew impatient and took her mouth properly, muffling her protests, going hard and insistent, then tasting her, licking her. Such ripe delicious lips. The best food of all to devour was the mouth of his lover.

Then he fed her some more, but this time he alternated food with playing with her breasts and her clit and scratching down her sides with his nails. He liked making her shudder. A few times she squeaked, and her breasts had the teeth marks to show for it.

"Pretty." He stroked one of the marks then lowered his head and sucked on her nipple, drawing all of it deep within his mouth, flicking at the nub with his tongue. She shuddered and her juices wet his thigh where she sat.

Letting her sit there while he only caressed her and stroked her made her become ever more aroused. Her nipples were tight buttons, her cunt swollen and so prepared for sex he could sink two fingers into her with ease…she merely shut her eyes and arched. The clever thing was controlling her responses.

But he wanted to hear her if she came.

He took his mouth off her, extracted his fingers, and jiggled his thigh. "Hop up. Kneel in front of me. You can make sounds if you want to."

Her expectant demonic look made him lounge back against the chair and wait.

She knelt, elegantly.

"I can make sounds?" She quirked up one brow.

"You can. And you can take me in your mouth."

"Oh? What if I don't want to?"

Ahh. The game ratcheted up a notch. A thrill traveled through him. Though she dodged, he seized the back of her hair in one fist. "Then, I make you." He shook her head, seeing with glee how that also shook her elsewhere. Things wobbled on females. With steady force, he dragged her forward, made her open and take the head of his cock into her mouth.

Feigned reluctance? Yes. Her butt shifted and she hummed happily as she rode his cock all the way down, engulfing him with her moist lips.

Gods. Pleasure rocketed through him. Up and down, he watched her take him. She curled her tongue around the shaft and cupped his balls with her hands. The tip of her tongue traced around the head of his cock and he hissed out a forbidden curse. What male wouldn't like this?

A game, this was a game they both seemed to instinctively know. Her challenging, him responding and making her.

There was only one thing he wanted more. And so, when he was about to erupt into her mouth he dragged her head up, made her stand and then instructed harshly. "Sit on me."

"You're so insistent." She tilted her head and put her hands over his where they held her hips. "And if I say no?"

Fiery determination arrived. He twisted her around in spite of her squeals and protests. He slapped her ass hard, far harder than he ever had in play with Nasskia, and he forced her down until his cock probed at her softest, most intimate place.

"Fuck," she muttered, as he sank into her. He could see his cock disappearing, impaling her. This, *this*, was what he desired. In. More. His thighs met her ass. The squeeze of her pussy muscles was sweet and tight.

He'd penetrated into her as far as he was able to and had, in some way he didn't comprehend, made her an indelible part of him.

With his chin resting atop her head, and both arms hugging her to him, he whispered the stupidest words he'd ever said, "I wish I could keep you forever."

Her reply stunned him.

Chapter 12

Willow groaned and clutched at his arms. She was anchored to his lap and couldn't get up. When a man was inside her this deep, when it was this first moment, she was often overcome with wonder.

She moaned and put her hand between her legs, making a *V* of her fingers, to feel the shaft of his cock and how it went up into her. How wet she was. She was him and he was her. One beautiful being. Only with Stom it seemed a hundred times multiplied. When he moved in her she wasn't sure about the heavens moving but maybe an orchestra played a few damn symphonies.

She leaned back into his body as he rocked her faster on his thighs. Pleasure grew.

He'd said words. *I wish I could keep you forever.* Those words filtered in, and she, caught up in this moment of elation, of union, of raw, hot, jaw-dropping sex, she reacted without thinking, and she murmured back to him her words. They were crazy words that she wanted to take back as soon as she said them.

"Me too."

Yet she meant them, with all her heart, and with every morsel of her being.

He gasped and hugged her tighter, his arms wrapped below her breasts. "We have to talk. After."

With what he was doing down below, where he'd slipped his hand over hers, to play in her moisture and even worm the tip of one of his fingers into her, alongside his cock, she was lucky to manage a whimper in reply.

"You like that?" He kept the finger in her while he screwed her slow and dirty, while he rotated her clit with his thumb and brought his other hand up to grip her throat. Then he said more soft beguiling words that reinforced his power.

He bit her and his cock speared up inside her like he wanted to find her mouth with the goddamned thing from the bottom up. Her clit throbbed, as if it would explode any second, and drove all proper thoughts away to the wilderness where logic dwelled at such times of momentous fucking.

When his hand went from her throat to her breasts, pinching them then delicately circling her nipples, one after the other, the pleasures tumbled together into one – the tugs on her nipples, the bites of his teeth, the fondling of her clit, the surge of impalement. She cried out, arching impossibly while she clawed at his arm and gasped her way through orgasm after echoing orgasm. Somewhere along the way, his own climax took him.

Smiling and sated, she listened to him struggle to bring down his breathing rate.

They stayed there together, on the chair, arms entwined, mouths gently kissing the beads of salty sweat from each other's skin. He remained inside her, and he stroked her hair and her sides, while their lust ebbed.

Reality trickled back in. On glancing down, she saw herself, which made this even more surreal. The orgasm had cleared her mind. She slipped off his lap to her knees.

When she heard him lean in behind her, she covered her breasts with her hands.

"What is it?" he asked, caressing her hair again.

"I'm insane," she whispered.

"Why would you say that?"

"If you're an alien, I must be. If you're not, I am anyway." She stayed hunched over a little, so he couldn't see her but something alerted him.

"Then I'm insane too. What are you hiding?"

She squeezed shut her eyes, not wanting to say, then looked at him, and gave in. "This." And she uncovered her breasts and her red nipples.

His eyes flared with interest. "Already? You're changing. Don't worry, it's not dangerous."

"What – You knew this would happen? I've got bright-red nipples, Stom! What's happening to me?"

"That is my red." His mouth tweaked upward. "It's the pet-creating nano-chem I gave you. Your lips are changing color too. It means you're mine."

What in holy fuckedness did that mean?

She blinked, licked her lips, and checked herself out again. Red, as in very. "I'm yours?" A happy glow kindled inside her, and she whispered, "I am crazy. I am." She made herself look at Stom but he only raised his brow and smiled. "I feel happy about this. Proud even. That is…so stupid with a big *S*."

"For a pet, that's normal. Me, it makes me want to do things. It makes me want to touch you there." He sucked in an enormous breath. "I want so many things. I want to make you mine forever, just as I said, yet I know I can't. And you," he reached forward and traced the inside of her ear, and she had to make herself resist crawling back onto his lap. "You must have many questions. I also know that you're craving me." A smug smile crept the corners of his mouth upward.

Bastard.

But, she did crave him and she whined her distress then pulled at her hair. "This is so bloody *wrong*!"

Miserable, she pouted. If he wasn't an alien, he had messed with her head real good. But she had very few doubts anymore. This was more concrete evidence than she even wanted. Her nipples had been normal a half hour ago. Now they were frickin *red*.

"I agree. Though right now, looking at you, I'm so conflicted." He scrubbed his face with both hands. "Let's go shower again. Then, I promise, we can talk about this properly."

"Wait. So you did give me something? A what, a nano-chem?"

He nodded, looking unhappy.

"I should be wanting to kill you, but I don't. Why?" Tears of frustration ran down her cheeks. She sniffed them back. "Okay. Shower, but promise we will just sit down after and talk. *No sex.*"

He nodded. "I promise. But only if you let me cuddle with you."

"The big bad alien wants a cuddle?" she asked, incredulous.

He growled.

"Fine! Okay. Done. Let's fucking cuddle." Then she eyed his torso and those muscles, secretly breathed in that essence of *him*, and sighed. Who was she kidding? He'd have to beat her off with a stick.

This time she walked up the stairs with him, her hand in his enormous one, with this man who might or might not be an alien. Except now she was certain. She peeked at how the black stripes on his skin seemed to flow with the movement of his muscles. They were all over him, curling over his chest, tickling down into his groin, even looping around his balls. He was. An alien.

But at least he was *her* alien.

They showered together, excruciatingly careful not to bump into each other too much. Every time they did, accidentally, touch, it was electric. Her nipples were sticking out like little pressable buttons by the time they were done. Toweling herself down with the big soft towel was an erotic exercise.

She shook her head and followed his alien majesty's incredibly sexy ass to the king-sized bed then gingerly sat at the foot of it. Stom sat at the top, against the headboard, and stretched out his legs for a million miles on the black quilt. From the look of his erection he was as painfully aware of her as she was of him.

She chuckled, grinning. "Guess this chem has made you all horny too?"

Though he glowered, after a second he shook his head in amusement. He beckoned. "Remember? Cuddle."

"Fuck. No." She swallowed. She'd never keep her hands off him like that. Or him off her. "I can't."

Squirming was like an advertisement saying she was aroused, but she couldn't stop squeezing her thighs together and doing a tiny butt wiggle. She frowned at his smirk.

"I'm sorry, Willow. I promise we will just talk, but I need to touch you. Please."

Who was lying to who here? "Fine."

She crawled up the bed and wriggled into his side.

For a while they simply stayed like that, together, slowly enfolding into each other, and yes, touching. She'd never had a lover like this – one who felt so right to her in every way. Now that they weren't making love, he treated her as if she were something precious.

Though they'd agreed not to be overly affectionate, they both quietly explored the other. She smelled his neck, licked a short distance along one of the black stripes on his chest where it tucked beneath his arm, and she reached up to trace the curves and marks of his face. Fascinating. As if he wanted not to scare her, for the most part Stom only stroked her back or her hair, but he watched her and sometimes smiled when she hesitated.

His tug on her hair made her look up.

"I won't bite."

"I know. You're just," she shut her eyes, "just a bit intimidating. And I don't...I can't see what happens to us after this. I'm scared of that."

"Yes. Me also. Take your time. I have you until the end of the day, only after that, must I return you."

Even that was a surprise. He had to let her go, soon. Had to. Yet he assumed she was his until then. At this piece of information, relief slid in, as well as foreboding.

Finally she stopped and curled her toes and thought of what to ask. Then she sat up on her heels, like a good schoolgirl about to do a class presentation, and she cleared her throat.

"Okay." She tsked. Beginning was hard to do. "Can you start? Tell me something."

"Very well. I'll try. We're a conglomeration of starfaring races, and though we try to be good and fair to the lesser races, we also have an enemy called the Bak-lal who would like to take all other intelligent races and make them like they are."

"Who?"

"The Bak-lal. They have been here, on Earth. We came to see if your race can become starfarers because that's the only way you can ever defend yourselves against them. And we found they had been here first."

"Okay." She thought. "That makes no sense to me." Her fingernails ended up curled into her thighs. Logically, what the hell was he doing with her? "Why this? Me. What's this got to do with anything?"

"Our command uses the pets as indicators as to whether you can become starfarers. The same chem tests you to see if you can ever be wormhole travelers."

"And we can?"

"Yes. If you can be pets, you can."

The vital question, for her, remained unanswered. "Sooo, it's decided already. Why *me*. What about me?"

"You." He sat forward, feral gleam in his gaze. "You are my reward for battle success. You're a gift I may earn. A beautiful woman who will become my pet if I so wish to chase you down."

Struck dumb by his intensity, her mouth open in an *O* of astonishment, she tried to gather a witty reply. She swallowed past her dry throat. "Am not."

He burst into laughter. "You're not? Willow, if you were trying to keep me from thinking about fucking you, that was the wrong way to do it. Sitting like that before me." He nodded at her body. "I can see your breasts and how they are marked with my color." Now he angled his left upper arm her way, where his red spiral was carved into his arm. "Like this. You match."

"Oh." She compared the two. She did match him. A perfectly exact shade.

Then he pointed at her pussy. "And there."

"What?" She edged her thighs closer together.

"I can still see you. You're marked there also, as you should be."

She looked down and saw how her clit and the very edge of her slit showed. Both were red. "Fuck me dead," she said, awed.

"Really?" Then he grabbed her legs and flipped her onto her back, swarmed up her, and spread her open using his body. He leaned over her and held her hands to the bed near her waist.

"Stop looking!" This was so embarrassing. Trying to close her legs only drove home to her how impossible that was when he wanted them open. "This will fade, yes?"

"No, even if I do nothing more to you, the marking will stay. According to our laws, you are nine tenths my property. I need but follow through with the last stage of capture. I release you, I capture you, I fuck you one last time. And then, you would be mine. Only Feya honor holds me back." He searched her eyes as if he could find an answer there.

The power of those words made her ache with want. "Only nine tenths? Ha-ha."

"Mmm. I'd lick you here except I promised not to. Such a pretty cunt. You're so tempting, little bitch. All red. All mine."

Fuck.

No. Don't think of him licking there. Or of his tongue. Her eyes were probably like saucers. She floundered and blurted, "No calling me bitch, thank you."

But the *all mine* and the growly possessiveness in his voice had made her dampen instantly. She'd felt the moisture wetting her lower lips. She prayed he'd not seen anything.

In her mind she saw herself bound in chains and silken scraps, kneeling at Stom's feet. In his hand was a leash linked to a red collar around her neck, and her mouth was open, already swallowing his cock as he forced it into her.

The fantasy was as solid as rock.

Damn it.

Not me, she tried to tell herself. Then she gasped at the pressure of something blunt nudging between her spread open legs.

The real Stom, here and now, was above her smiling with deliciously nasty intent and his cock was a moment away from being inside her. Just a little more.

"Heyy," she said softly, hoping he'd keep going.

Still pinning her, but shifting his knees back, he lowered his head, put his tongue on her, then luxuriously licked, from the middle of her slit to her clitoris.

"Ummm. Oh fuck. Unfair." She exhaled and lowered her eyelids.

On that perfect spot, he did slow arousing circles on her clit with his tongue tip.

"Ohh." She flopped her head back and groaned, pushing her pussy up at him.

She could tell how he was toying with her there – knew exactly what his amazing tongue did, every dab, every flick, every suck, and was also aware of where his hands fastened her wrists to the bed. The head of his cock had for a fleeting moment pressed into her entrance. She remembered, she wanted him in her, *now*.

Then he stopped.

"More, or not, little pet? Would you rather I bite you?" Then he carefully took her clit between his teeth. "Hmm?"

"Not that! More of –" She raised her head, half-afraid he meant to bite. He let go, licked her once then bit again. "The other," she choked out.

"Then stay still. Say 'yes, Stom'."

She barely hesitated. "Yes, Stom. Please."

"Good. I like the please."

"Mmm." She writhed on him and his tongue wetly teased her and began to slowly drive her insane.

She'd had lovers who were good at cunnilingus but something about their relationship, their pure attraction and the way he made her be still while he played, elevated what Stom did to a devastating art. He didn't seem to care how long he aroused her for.

She came once, and he kept going. *No. No, no.* By then he'd released her hands. She tried to clutch at his hair to pull him away but he growled.

Admonished, she flopped back and found her concentration focusing on what his mouth was doing.

Slowly, her arousal reassembled.

Oh, his fucking glorious mouth.

Pleasure and heat built again, pumping up to that oblivious almost, *almost* there state, where the angels came down from the heavens, and time stood still.

More, more, please more. Tongue. Mouth. More licking. And he wouldn't let her go.

Lust, pure mind-altering, muscle-shaking lust, owned her body in an incandescent storm, blasting away her mind in climax. After that, he held her tighter, as if knowing she would struggle, which she did, then he made her come again. Though she strived to wrap her legs around his body and wrench him away, he was too strong. Panting, squealing at his insistent touch, she found herself overcome.

After the third time she begged for him to stop.

Exhausted, through slitted eyelids and the sweat beading on her lashes, she watched him crawl up to her and smile triumphantly.

"Now we are done, sweet pet. Happy?"

She grunted at him and patted his shoulder with a hand that slid off and down his rock-sculpted biceps. "Yes."

Then he flopped down beside her and snuggled her into him, spooning. His cock prodded at her back.

"You?" she asked.

"Later, girl, I will take you. For now, you're mine and going nowhere. Rest."

She should argue that. Normally she would, but she only smiled and let him clasp her hand and kiss her fingers. She drew his to her mouth and kissed them too, though she could smell herself on them. "Thank you, Stom."

His sigh seemed to merge into his words, as if her hearing had warped. "If you were truly mine forever, I'd make you call me Sir."

If.

The world cracked a little. He hadn't said that he wanted her to say it now, it wasn't that. Right then she'd have done anything for him. Rather it was that with that single *if* he'd negated all that had come before. Her eyes watered.

The *mine* had been temporary.

She should have known. She should have been sensible. Well, she had known, but she'd conveniently forgotten for a while. She'd never been going to leave Ally over some temporary alien boyfriend. Even if he'd just won an Olympic medal for oral. The fantasy, though, it had been so good, so all-encompassing and so real.

Feeling suddenly alone, despite his skin on hers, and his lips at her nape, she stared at the empty bed before her and the messed-up sheets.

"There's more, isn't there, Stom? We both have more to say."

Silence.

"Yes."

In her head she began bringing back her real life. Ally. Leaving the house. Training to be a firefighter. This followed this, followed that. None of her plans had alien lovers in them.

"I can't ever leave Ally alone. She's helpless and impossible but I love her. I will always protect her. Do you see? And –" She shook her head, frowning. "I can't imagine making her go with an alien man, just so I could be with you." *Ick.* That seemed terrible, even if she'd been one step away from falling at Stom's feet.

"That can't happen anyway. The Preyfinders select women carefully. Only those who…"

"What?" She sensed something important here, had felt his muscles tense. "Tell me. I was selected. Why?"

Still he said nothing.

"What is it?"

Stom sighed. "Very well. You need to make a choice. Though I don't know what to do, really I don't. I can't keep you because I was bond mated. Feya don't ever have more than one mate. I vowed Nasskia would be my only love after she died and…even taking a pet negates that vow." He rolled away.

When she turned over, she found him flat on his back, staring at her in misery. "That I can't stop touching you is unforgivable. I don't understand my own reactions."

Time ticked slowly past. "You're like me, but you shouldn't be?"

"I think so. Though I've never been a pet, so I'm not sure." Stom gave a cut-off laugh. "You're a compulsion. Even now." His gaze wandered over her.

"What a pair we are. Yes. That's me too. I hate that you've done this, but I…" Her forehead wrinkled. She almost loved him. She wished she could ease his pain even, could find a true path through this for them both.

"I wish this wasn't such a mess, but me, I wouldn't go with you anyway. Ally is not just my responsibility or a thing I have to do. She's my cousin, and I'm all she has left. We've gone through so much together. Her mother's death. My parents. Her illness. I will *never* desert her. Apart from putting her in an institution, there's only me, or living in a share house with many others with mental problems." She shuddered. "Even with the best assistants in those, I've heard of bad things happening to women."

"I see. I understand that and respect you for it. Only there is that one detail you asked me to say." He paused then went on, the words rolling out. "Why you were chosen. You're dying, Ally. Kasper plans to kill you, but also, you have Aids and not just a plain variety. You'll die within a few years, even with the best treatment you humans can muster. If I took you, you would be cured." The sadness in his eyes was terrible in its depth.

"I what? This is crazy. I have Aids?" She almost didn't hear the rest. Her mind was buzzing, blanking out with too much noise.

"Yes." He lay back again and wiped his hands down his face. His voice cracked. "Perhaps I can take you with me and afterward, after you're healed, give you to another. But I doubt it. The laws to do with lesser races are strictly enforced."

And if he did that, Ally would be alone. Maybe she'd die too. She bit her hand. *Oh hell.*

I'm dying.

"Willow? Do you want me to try?"

Her answer slurred out. She wasn't concentrating. "Do what?"

"See if I can take you as a pet, but hand you to another? Once you're cured. Brask mentioned it might be possible."

The idea was startling. "Then I could return here?"

"No. If another made you their pet, you would be theirs." He remained staring at the ceiling, his words as dry as a forest of bones. "Always theirs."

She sprang off the bed. "Then no. Fuck no. Take me home now, please."

God he was beautiful.

Stom sat up and came to her, standing there with his fists clenched at his sides. "I mustn't forget why I brought you here – to convince you to leave before Kasper comes for you."

"You think he will?" She wiped her eyes with the back of her hand.

"I know he is."

"I'm going. I am. I will." When he glared at her, she spat back, "I will! Now, take me back." *Asshole.*

The contrast was ripping into her heart – between lust, disgust, and whatever this feeling was that she had for this stupid alien. She hated him, and she wanted to collapse on him and bawl her eyes out.

She'd be strong. She had a few years, he'd said, as long as she avoided Kasper. Somehow she'd find somewhere good to leave Ally. Before she… How? How could she be dying? It wasn't fair!

Be sensible. Get some blood tests. Make sure it's true. But she knew, already, that he wasn't lying.

That had really put a dampener on the day. Inside her heart was cold and she could barely lift her feet as she followed him to another room to get new clothes.

He could have told her those facts the moment he brought her back here, instead of having crazy monkey sex with her. That part, on thinking some more, she forgave him for.

The drive to the house was lonely. Neither of them spoke until they stood outside the car and he was about to go.

"No more burning anything. Leave here tomorrow. Keep that near you." He nodded at the bag that she held. Once she'd promised she would run from Kasper, he'd returned the gun to her.

"I won't need it here. The house is safe."

"Nowhere near Kasper is safe. I have to be on a shuttle tonight to catch the next warp ship. I can't watch you anymore. I have to officially give up that right."

"You don't understand. This house is safe. Nothing bad has ever happened while we're inside." She'd been on the brink of telling him why before and his look of misery had tipped the balance. She could reassure him. What would it matter if he knew? Besides, the longer they talked, the longer she could put off him going. "It does *something* to people who want to harm us. They forget. They just…go away. In like fifteen years I've seen boyfriends, crims, do that. Once a whole riot went past and we were like a rock in front of a waterfall. They went around us. Nothing touches this house."

Slowly his face had cleared. Sadness morphed to puzzlement. "Okay. That's good."

"Yes, it is."

She blinked, feeling that throb in the middle of her forehead grow. What was she doing? He was the best man she'd ever met, and she was letting him slip away just because he was an alien?

Crap. No, it wasn't that. Not anymore. She didn't care what he was. It was Ally. Her and Ally were like twins. And it was him and his past. His dead wife stood in the way.

"You be good too."

Her lips trembled. The awful tension between the here and the now, and what would soon be true, strained at her until she was sure her heart was about to tear into a hundred pieces. "Yes. I will."

He touched her cheek before getting back in the car. She could still feel the line of his caresses on her skin.

As the car drove away, she stared after it blindly. Tears rolled down her face. The wind stirred her hair.

She was going to miss him so much.

When she went through the door, Ally greeted her with two cupped handfuls of daisies and a scream as she flung her arms around her in a hug. The daisies went flying.

"Where have you been? Willow?"

"Places. Visiting a friend." She patted the girl's back and smiled. "Let's get dinner going."

Her nose screwed up. "The fridge smelled and I threw out some stuff. There mightn't be much to eat."

"Ah. I'll find something."

That night she began packing. There was only one place she could think of to go – a friend in Bundaberg. Ally found her doing it and stood in the doorway scowling, with her arms folded, for at least five minutes.

"Shoo. It's only temporary."

"Don't believe you." She walked away.

"Me neither." But she blew her nose and kept packing.

Chapter 13

In the morning, on that horrible, excruciating morning, after waking and trudging through to the kitchen while yawning and scratching at her intensely itchy arm, she felt the absence, a strange lack of personality. The house was too quiet. She walked then ran from room to room and found Ally was gone.

The yard too was empty.

She went and dressed in practical jeans and T-shirt then grabbed the gun and her phone just in case Ally had hers. She wasn't sure where the girl kept her mobile phone or if it was charged, but she might have it even if she hadn't answered it yet.

That was all she could think of. She might have to call the cops if she couldn't find her. Where the girl would go, she had zero idea. She hadn't been outside their house and yard by herself for years, apart from the rare doctors' visits and they were carefully arranged.

There was one place actually. The reservoir.

She went outside.

Heart thumping, she walked to the steel ladder going up to the side of the cylindrical reservoir. Funny but she'd had a text confirming she could take her in for reassessment tomorrow. If she found her, the girl was attending that one for sure. She'd run away for chrissakes. How was she going to cope with car travel all the way to Bundaberg?

Again, she'd have to delay leaving. It'd be worth it. But first, find her.

"This is going to be a nightmare." She swept her hair back into a tiny ponytail, arranged the little shoulder bag that held the gun, and started up the ladder. The rungs clanged under her gym shoes. "When I find you Ally, I am giving you a piece of my mind."

She paused a few feet up and swallowed down a bad taste. The piece of mind might have to wait until after she breathed into a paper bag for a while, metaphorically. Her stomach was hurting like she'd eaten acid and broken glass. She kept going, climbed up the last few steps and looked across the flat concrete roof of the reservoir. The wind gusted hard up here and the sun seemed hotter and closer. She squinted, hoping stupidly. Nothing to see, and she'd known that in point five of a second really. Ally wasn't here. Grit crackled under the soles of her shoes.

There was a steel trapdoor that must lead down into the water itself. For inspections or water testing, they'd guessed. It had never opened. Locked, every time they'd ever tried it. But something made her stomach give an extra roll as she looked down on it. Dread crawled in. She stooped and pulled on the handle.

It didn't budge.

"Fuck." She put her head in her hands for a moment. In the back of her mind had been the idea that Ally might do something really stupid. Really, really stupid, like suicide. She put her palms together in the prayer position and looked up at the blue sky. "Thank you."

Walking around the circumference of the roof, Willow scanned the local neighborhood, though already despairing. No splattered body below. Again, thank god. The girl could be anywhere.

But, considering who she was, she'd likely not go too far. The roofs of the houses below were separated by roads with cars, by footpaths strewn with people, by yards of houses with more people…lots of people. The forest between here and the park looked like a green people-free zone by contrast. Ally territory. The wind shook the thick foliage like a giant had swept his palm over the tops of the trees. She'd try there first, then maybe some of the quieter streets. After that, fucked if she knew. Cops?

She should've sat down with her last night and at least tried to prepare her. Damn being love sick. She sniffed. Then for a minute she allowed herself to cry, just let the tears pour out. She'd never been a crier before him – had just gotten on with life, forged through, shouldered things. He'd made her expect someone to help her through the bad times, because she knew he would've done that, if he could've. If he hadn't decided she was not worth keeping.

"Dumbass," she told herself.

She wiped her face with her arm and started down the ladder. The twinges in her stomach reminded her she'd not had breakfast. Maybe do a straight through the middle search to the park then do the edges? Then kinda criss-cross the whole forest again?

By the time she was ten yards under the trees, she was thinking more of antacid medicine than food. Crap. She paused and held her hand over her stomach. Way to go. Having food poisoning or a stomach ulcer was not what she needed, today of all days.

The crunch of dead leaves over to the left had her twitching her gaze there. A lizard? Shadows flitted across. Tall shadows. No six-foot lizards here, that she knew of. Fuck. Not again. Last time she'd shot Stom. Maybe this was some homeless guy? More noises, definite footsteps, to the right made her jump. Two homeless guys then. And another behind her, back in the direction of safety, and her house. Whoever it was, they meant her to hear. When they moved in, she walked faster toward the park, ready to run, her hand in the shoulder bag.

Someone chuckled. Leftie. From the right came the rattle of metal on metal.

Her stomach picked that moment to spear pains through her abdomen, enough to make her gasp. Her body exploded with red hurt.

Her vision blurred, speckled. Her ears rang. Her hands prickled with clammy heat. Giving up on shooting anyone, she released her grip on the gun and she ran, staggered, and blundered through the trees. Shrubs whipped at her ankles then swiped across her face. Something thudded on her knees. She had a mouth of dirt. Head muzzy with nausea and pain and all, she thought through the mud, and figured out she'd fallen. Everything whipped around in crazy incessant circles. Bile stung her throat.

They were coming for her and she couldn't even see. Or stand.

Chapter 14

Brask tapped his finger on the control circle on the screen and rolled the drone forward on the branch so it could have a better field of view. He wasn't here, officially, but he'd promised to keep an eye on Willow. Stom was one of those guys he found it hard to say no to. Better than he was morally. More able to connect with people than he was. Face it, helping the man would make him feel better than his normal, repugnant nastiness, for at least a half a day.

Willow's arm marking was curious. He'd snapped a pic of that and uploaded it in a message to Stom. In a way, he both prayed it was what he thought it was, and prayed it wasn't.

This stupid girl was not doing what Stom had told her to. She was searching for the other girl who had vanished overnight.

Most of his squad was over in the US wiping out the stray Bak-lals. He had zip to do except crawl around in this forest. Willow was a hundred yards away. Farther than he'd like but he was alone. He'd had to be careful about getting too close around the big reservoir since it was cleared land.

He leaned in. *Kak.* Three unidentified males were approaching her. He could either sprint and look damn obvious, or slink and maybe be useless if things went wrong.

Weapons, yeah, the screen metal-detecting overlay showed pistols, a few knives, a hacksaw, and a corkscrew. What? Who carried hacksaws and corkscrews? What were they planning to do to her?

His manpower resources were in the negative and he had a brawl going down. Sniping from back here was possible with a few homing rounds that could weave between the trees, but it wasn't allowed and he wasn't equipped anyway. He could take them all at close quarters, but he also wasn't allowed to help her exactly.

Rules were made to be upheld, not broken. He wasn't a rule breaker.

The screen showed her falling and tumbling into the leaf litter. The men moved in.

He snapped shut the drone control, threw it in his pocket, and sprinted. Getting to her before they did was a zero probability outcome. He needed the impossible. Stom was going to be shattered, even if he had discarded her. That marking on her arm looked most convincing.

Chapter 15

On the way up in the shuttle, he'd turned over what Willow had said about the house. The answer to why the house protected her, it was so obvious after what he'd heard from Brask about Dassenze and his suspicions about Earth women. Willow might not be a succubus, but she was doing something to the house, or to where it was. Same as Bambi cross Brittany could heal, she could protect. That had to be worth something to the Ascend? There, if he wanted to take the chance, was his way to get Ally cared for.

If.

All he had to do was to somehow get his rights to Willow reaffirmed. Convince Dassenze, the god assigned to Earth. Then take that last step. But would Nasskia forgive him if she knew? Could he throw aside that vow when it meant so much? Willow meant so much to him. That dilemma had occupied him all the way. Now that he was here, though…

This was ridiculous. Stom clutched at the bulkhead frame, then at his stomach as he lurched into sick bay. He never got ill. Not in a hundred warp ship flights.

"Take a seat there, sir." A medic pointed then hurried into the adjoining room.

He sat and, despite how he felt, he felt even sicker at having left Willow back there on Earth – by herself with Kasper after her. He was a coward after all. An honorable coward maybe, but still a coward.

An honorable stupid coward who had forsaken the one person alive who meant everything to him. He massaged his brow and decided. He was going back down to Earth.

The medic returned with a scanner. He sat next to Stom and smiled kindly. "Having a bit of trouble, are we?"

The room was swimming with blotches, his breakfast wanted to see the world again via his mouth, and this medic didn't deserve to be smacked, but he still growled.

"I have a headache that is sawing my head apart from the inside out. Stop talking to me."

"Mm-hm." The scanner whined as he passed it over Stom's head and chest. "Sir, I regret to inform you that you're too ill to go through a warp flight. Your blood chems are far from normal. It's odd. These enzymes are showing major organ damage building. Plus there's auto destruction of your blood cells occurring."

"Go away." He groaned and swallowed back some vomit. "I'm not that ill. And I'm not getting on the warp ship anyway."

"You are ill." That was a different voice.

Stom peered upward through his splayed fingers. A humanoid figure stood a few yards away, covered with an infinity of gleaming bronze scales. An Ascend, a god. Must be Dassenze. He should stand then bow, but he was going to fall off this chair if it kept moving. He merely nodded and grimaced. Then he lost track of where the god was as nausea built again.

"There is a message for you, Stom. One, I intercepted. They weren't going to give it to you straight away. You need to see it. Then I am returning you to Earth."

A holographic image appeared a few inches away. It was Willow climbing down a ladder on the side of the reservoir near her house. Gods, why was she there? The image zoomed in on her arm, showing a faint red spiral. He stared, unable to believe for several seconds. Elation arrived, followed by more disbelief.

"What? But...how can this be? I cannot have more than one bond mate."

"I believe you can. She is yours. As you are hers. These Earth females are extraordinary. Jadd's changed without the final dose, as has this one. She is not becoming a pet; she is becoming your bond mate. Your extreme sickness is also, I believe, the result of being parted from her."

"What? That's not normal. Nasskia and I...it never bothered me." He suppressed the urge to vomit again and swallowed. It wasn't smart to vomit on one's god, surely?

"I forgive your many *whats*, Stom. I can see you are dying. If I keep answering, I will end up talking to a corpse. Come. We return."

A fact popped up. "The shuttle has gone."

"Never fear. I will keep you safe as we re-enter the atmosphere."

"A spacesuit?" He hoped that was it. He'd need minutes to find one and be fitted but it was better than the alternative. The gods on occasion went out there in SpaceHardened mode. No suit. No nothing.

"No spacesuit. Try not to vomit on me." He took Stom's hand and smiled a godly smile that said bad things.

Oh kak. Stories said they had to use some weird god tubing on you that went down your throat and up you everywhere else as well as cocooning you.

He was a warrior. He would stay strong.

They went out through the airlock as one – him enclosed in an amber cocoon. He hoped his look of terror wasn't caught on surveillance camera. He screamed silently most of the way down. The world below was in darkness and their flight path took them in a shallow, high-velocity arc toward the brightness lining the horizon where the sun bathed the other half of the Earth.

As the atmosphere began to buffet them and the glow of heat flickered upon the forward parts of the amber cocoon, he saw that Dassenze had received a message. His speech vibrated through the glasslike cocoon to Stom.

"Willow is being attacked. Even I cannot reach her fast enough to stop this. Brask will get there before us yet is also too distant."

He couldn't speak but he blinked to show he'd heard what Dassenze had said. As long as they didn't mean to kill her instantly, there was hope.

Hope. His heart clenched and he said a prayer in his mind.

They screamed lower, flames burning off them, diving headfirst toward the surface of the planet.

Chapter 16

The lecture on the amplification of DNA from white blood cells had been as boring as picking paint colors, but not just because of the subject matter, which had very little new in it. The pull was there again, only this time *he* was close and it wasn't a vague tug, he was here, nearby. The man with the incisive green eyes. Talia could almost taste him.

At the end of the lecture, she strode out of the lecture theatre and headed for the car park, already texting Allan to say she wasn't going to make the lab work session. Her car was her Suzuki Swift that she'd had shipped in by train. As she spun the wheel to take her onto the motorway, she was grateful for her forethought. The sword in the trunk was a cheap modern version of a katana, but it felt right in her hand, even if the grip needed redoing.

The pull grew stronger as she neared Inala and she weaved down side streets until she reached a dead end. Bad neighborhood. Most of the houses looked tatty, their yards overgrown with grass and discarded car parts. Windows were busted, graffiti had taken over most flat surfaces, and half the shops she'd passed looked ready to fall down or be burgled.

She slammed the car door behind her; to the right was a towering gray concrete reservoir. Strange, it was the only structure that was clean – no graffiti.

She looked around. Nothing but kids playing. That mind-twisting *pull* teased her. He was here somewhere.

If she was crazy, this was when the men in white coats should come get her. Carrying a sword in public was enough to earn a criminal charge if she scared anyone, but she'd put a blanket in her trunk just for this sort of occasion. With the sword wrapped and tucked under her arm, she sauntered in the direction the pull took her – past a neat, white-fenced house and to the side of the reservoir. Here was a small forest – gray-trunked eucalypts and tallow wood trees.

She drew the sword and let the blanket flow to the ground. She breathed with her eyes half shut. Yes. Close. Like a wind beckoning. A purpose flowed into her and she became, not just a forensic biologist on sabbatical in a strange city who'd eaten too much sushi for dinner last night and had put on a few pounds, no, with that purpose, she became a warrior taken by a cause.

Her body moved toward what called her – dedicated in every muscle to arriving there without being heard or seen. Ridiculous and improbable given her upbringing, but this was her, her true being, with a sword in hand. Somewhere ahead was both her mystery and her destiny.

What she'd do when she reached him, she didn't know, but with something sharp in her hand, she was queen. Rock, paper, scissors, sword.

Every flicker of grass blade impinged on her consciousness, as did every warble and flutter of wing, every sway of branch, every shadow that darkened her surrounds. She'd never trained at anything but kendo but here, now, something had happened. She was ninja, astro boy, bat girl, and Uma Thurman from *Kill Bill*, on crack, with sprinkles on top.

Energy squeezed from her every cell, told her she was deadly, and she believed it. Fuck yeah.

Which was how she came across the three of them circling the woman on the ground like vultures who'd forgotten the last down payment on their wings. She stood at the edge of light and shadow, twirling her katana's point on the leather of her boot, watching them, and they had no clue.

It was possible she would have floated on by, sneaked flatfooted through the trees, because *he* was there, just on the other side of this small clearing. Possible – the pull was that bad.

Maybe this girl, who seemed unconscious, knew the men? Hey, who knew? Only when she stirred and mumbled, the tattooed one laughed and flipped her over onto her back. Another one, a tall guy with a red beard, dressed in biker leather, denim, and chains, pulled out a corkscrew.

What the hey?

Then the third, bald man drew a hacksaw from under his coat.

Etiquette said you introduced yourself, even if she had an urge to separate their heads from their torsos. Besides, it was a little illegal to behead people and so far all they'd done was gather around a flaked-out girl and show off their kitchen and man tools collection.

She took a deep breath and slowly walked over. Go, ninja girl.

"Hey guys, I'm all for kinky sex, but don't you think the hacksaw is taking it a little far?"

They turned and looked at her. Redbeard, baldie, and tattooed guy. She nodded to each of them.

Redbeard shrugged and stepped toward her. "We was just about to have fun. You wanna join in?" He nodded at her sword. "Think you can use that?"

The others spread out and began a classic encirclement.

"This?" She tilted the blade and sneered at it. "Picked it up in a junk sale."

Baldie, to her right, chuckled and she noted his position. Tattooed guy, still showing to the left, in her peripheral vision, dragged out a revolver and started speaking. "Hand over –"

The katana was point down but cutting edge up and theoretically that was good as she could sweep in one continuous motion. Samurai would keep their katanas ready in just such a position, only they had them tucked into their obi.

Hers was out and within lethal range of them all. They were unaware.

Strictly speaking, legally, she couldn't say they'd done more than frighten her, and so deadly force wasn't allowed. She could hit them and run, but she couldn't do anything really bad...

He continued his speech. "...the sword."

Redbeard unslung a chain to go with his corkscrew.

The barrel of the revolver cleared Tattooed guy's coat opening and was swinging out.

No deadly force until he shot her?

Fuck this.

In one arc, starting on the left, she sliced through Tattooed guy's throat, which meant carotid artery spurt...*damn the blood spray would get her*...severed Redbeard's wrist then on the reverse arc, separated Redbeard's head from his neck...*using a corkscrew on a girl, jeez.* There was a *crack* and a *spang.*

In the air, a blade spun, flinging glints of light.

As she swiveled to deal with Baldie, she recognized the sounds and the altered feel of the katana for what it was – the blade had snapped, one inch from the grip. Her left hand reached out at speed.

Well that was a bad buy. But at least her astro-ninja-batgirl instincts were working. She'd grabbed the blade with her left hand and now held it like an Olympic torch gone wrong. Shouldn't that be hurting? The thing was sharp as well as cheap.

Baldie gaped at her, with a mother fucking huge cannon of a gun pointed her way. But beyond him was an onrushing man in a coat. Him, her brain screamed. *Him, him, him.*

Yeah, I get it. Whatever part of her was doing the proximity alert, it needed to turn down the volume. Maybe these guys were all together? Crap. No, please, not Coatman.

With the snapped-off blade in her left hand, she spiked Tattooed guy clean through the nose and up into the cribriform plate that separated nose and brain. Things went *splurt*. She was amazed when *A* her left hand that held the naked blade didn't split in half and *B* the blade came out again like she'd plunged it into spaghetti and not skull and brain.

Maybe she was Bladegirl not ninjagirl? Names needed deciding.

Again the man had possessed the hacksaw, ergo, he deserved dying, muchly.

He was collapsing already and likely dead, when her cute, scary, green-eyed guy, currently known as Coatman, came leaping over the top, his hand outstretched, gun in it.

A flash recall told her letting him grab her neck was bad. She dodged and made to cut his leg, just a little, only to find her arm had turned to rock. She couldn't cut him, but she could dance. Her agility was still there. With a swerve and a duck, she slipped away.

The man rolled and came up on his feet. He tucked the gun away under his long black coat.

There was blood everywhere. Forensics would have a field day with this. Blood spatter, severed fucking heads, corkscrews. While still keeping a wary eye on…

"Who are you?" she demanded, eyes narrowing. "I know you."

I've travelled for a thousand miles to find you.

This man she'd searched for had a simple presence most men never achieved. Self-assured and wide, yet she'd bet all of him under that partly open coat was muscle. Sandy hair that glinted gold at the tips and a squarish, rugged face.

She had an itch to trace the creases there and ask him where he got those awesome blue cheek tattoos. Like shark gills or something. They'd even been shaded so they looked carved in.

"You remember me? Curious. My name is Brask. I came to help her. Though technically, I shouldn't." He gestured at the girl who had curled up into a ball. "And you, you need me to help you clean up all this. They're dead. Your world doesn't like people getting dead, do they?"

"My world?"

"What else do you remember, apart from me in general?" The deep sexy purr of his voice struck low and made her long-neglected lady bits quiver warmly to life. This Brask could have been a beast in another life.

She had to do a slow shuffle and step to keep him distant. He seemed determined to close the gap, and whenever she stepped away, he followed.

"Not much. I don't remember anything much at all. Stay there, please. I've got this." She brandished the broken sword in her bloodied fist.

He halted and cocked one eyebrow. "Shouldn't that have cut you? Can I see your hand? And I've got a gun, by the way. Gun trumps sword."

"Not in my world," she muttered. Funny how both of them were sparring despite all the dead, like they were immune or something. She'd never thought herself callous. Later, she had a feeling all this was going to crash down on her. She gave her mind a metaphorical shake. "No, you can't see my hand. Help her, and stop stalking me."

He grunted dismissively but bent then went to one knee and peered at the girl. While he did that, she spread her palm. Blood, but not hers. No cuts. None. This was freaky.

"She seems to be recovering. I can't touch her to be sure. Willow, if you can hear me, Stom is coming."

"Stom? Is that her boyfriend? Weird name. Why can't you touch her? Step back and I'll check her out."

"Stom is not her boyfriend, Talia. He's her bond mate and possibly her Master." He smiled oddly as he said that, as if he knew something she didn't. "They're coming soon so you needn't touch her. Don't be surprised."

"Uh-huh." What an odd thing to say. All of that had been. The sensual menace radiating from this Brask was affecting her. It was exhilarating. Such a scary yet fascinating game. Playing mysteries with a man who'd watched her kill three other men and not batted an eyelid.

"You're not scared of me, are you?" she asked gently.

"No." He laughed.

"Maybe you should be."

"I doubt that. Maybe you should be scared of me, Talia." He took a step nearer and in the face of what she'd just told him, she stood her ground. Damn, the man had grown some inches.

Chasing this guy was like following a hurricane, and holding onto its tail.

Her name. He'd said it before. "How do you know my name?"

"Because. I'll tell you, if you tell me why you're here."

Shit. He'd put his finger on the anomaly.

"Really? You swear?"

"I do, and I never break my word."

It seemed, in that instant, that finding out how he knew her name was the secret to end all secrets. They'd met before and he was about to say how.

But the reason why she decided to tell him wasn't just to get his answer; it was because this had become a sexual game. And what she would say was going to up the stakes.

"I'm here because I knew you would be. I've been tracking you, Brask."

He swallowed and his eyes widened. "How?"

That wasn't in the contract they'd just made, but she told him. "I can feel where you are."

He froze at that. The type of freeze that said he wanted to conceal how he felt about what she'd said. And that, alone, provoked her to tease him. Very slowly, she smiled in a way that said, *gotcha*.

Brask replied, narrow lipped and nasty. "I know your name because I've met you before, on the rooftop apartment where your sister used to live. I know where she is now. She's alive and happy, but you know what makes me happy? That I then made you forget. I can do what I like with you, Talia."

Shit. She quailed a little. Was that the truth? This man was more dangerous than she'd imagined. But, Brittany was alive? Nothing could best that, or so she thought.

Not until a flaming comet appeared in the sky and plummeted to the earth at her feet, and two men stepped forth. One of them was covered in bronze scales. A glance from his golden eyes made the world about her fade and her knees weaken.

She stared until a hand grasped her neck.

"Thought that would distract you." Brask looked into her eyes.

A powerful jolt swept her and she collapsed to her knees. When she tried to rise, the jolt hit her again.

"You're so resistant to this, miss. I'd love to know why. Sleep. Forget."

She remembered laying a hand on his at the angle of her shoulder, and the flash striking her again at the same time as a wave of goose bumps.

"I need to get a new strategy. The *look* isn't working with you. You may not like it, but I can't have you tracking me in this out-of-control state, no matter how good you are with a sword."

Blackness closed in. She'd done this before, hadn't she?

Chapter 17

At least Dassenze had spared him the embarrassment of arriving in that cocoon with tubes up him everywhere. *Ouch.*

Stom staggered over to where Willow lay. His legs wobbled. Slowly and in as dignified a way as he could, he collapsed next to her. Face to face he could see her paleness.

"You sick too, sweet girl?" He draped his arm over her and pulled her into his chest. Stroking her cheek and saying soft words of encouragement made her eyelids stir. Strength was pumping back into him by the second, so it was likely she'd be recovering soon.

"Stom?" she whispered.

"Yes. Me. I'm back, and this time I'm not leaving you."

"Good." Her smile lit up her face and landed a big lump of sorrow in his chest.

He'd been ill when he arrived, but not so ill he hadn't seen the carnage around her. He owed Brask. Those men must've planned to do bad things to his girl.

"I'm so sorry, Willow. I never meant this to happen. I guess I'm plain stupid."

"Yep." Her smile turned into a weak grin. Seeing her lift her eyelids and her brown eyes emerge made it worthwhile. "Are you the reason I feel like shit?"

"I am." He kissed her softly. "We're bond mates. You have my mark on your arm now too."

"The squiggly thing you have?" Her frown wasn't the best sign. Neither was the shake in her voice. "I thought my arm was itchy."

"Why are you frowning?"

Willow searched his face. "You only came back because of a mark on my arm?"

"Oh, no. No, no, no." While he used his thumb to smooth the corrugation from between her brows, he rustled up an answer. "I was returning anyway. Once I arm wrestled a god into letting me. I figured out how to keep Ally out of trouble. Which meant you couldn't say no anymore. You're more important than you think and I can use you for leverage. That, plus I need you. A lot." That lump in his chest got painful. Dumb explanation. Need wasn't the right word but it was the best he could manage.

"Uh-huh. I'm leverage now?" Her grumble was more like the old Willow. "I can't say no? Betcha I can."

He sighed, decided the new pinkness meant she was well enough, so he kissed her. When he'd coaxed her to kiss him back, and was sure she was happier, he pulled away an inch.

"Hmm. So you'd arm wrestle a god for me?"

A deep voice cut in. "I'm sure he would have, though I was more concerned about Stom being sick on me. And yes, he'd already decided not to board the warp ship before he found out you were bonded."

They both looked up at Dassenze. The bronzed god waited with an impatient air.

He'd forgotten they were being observed. Stom crawled to his knees so he could help Willow rise.

Dassenze continued, "What you need to understand, Willow, is that love is guaranteed once you are bonded. I just wish brains were also. Considering your extreme withdrawal symptoms, I would imagine you and Stom's love for each other is equally intense. Neither of you are allowed beyond this solar system until I investigate that. Your friend, Ally, she's in a cave of vegetation in the culvert next to your house. Now, if you'll excuse me, I have that war a few systems away to attend to."

Love? Huh. Was that the word he meant? It seemed a little beyond the boundary of how he'd describe their relationship.

Dassenze stalked off and Stom watched Willow's eyebrows come down from way high, and her open mouth slowly close.

"It's okay, he's not really angry with you." He took her elbow to steady her as she unfolded her legs.

"What is he? A reptile race or something?" She very carefully dusted off her jeans, as if she was trying not to draw attention to something else.

Stom choked back a snort. "No. Dassenze is a god, an Ascend. The scales don't mean he's a lizard. He aids us, within limits."

"A god? Really? That's…wow, just wow." She paused. "Ascend. As in climb? Does that mean he was once ordinary?"

"Clever of you. Some believe that."

"I bet." The sudden paling of her skin hinted that she wasn't quite well. He grabbed her arm again.

From the increased luminosity of his scales, Dassenze was about to launch at any second, yet he'd paused to look down at the woman who was sprawled off to the side. Brask had been checking on her and as Dassenze showed interest, Stom would've sworn the man bristled. He'd seen Feya mock fight over potential bond mates many times and these two gave off that same dominant and competitive male aura. Well, well. Interesting.

"Who is she?" Willow asked.

"I don't know."

"Do your gods have sex, I mean…"

"Do they ever fuck women from your planet? The answer is yes."

"Hmm. Then I hope she has a cast iron vagina."

At that he couldn't help bursting into laughter. Luckily Dassenze took off heavenward before he could have heard and became a rapidly dwindling gold speck in the sky. Stom scooped the protesting Willow into his arms, angling her so she was unlikely to see the bodies.

"Come. I'm taking you home. We'll find Ally, and then –" He pecked her on the nose. "I have to plan the last official stage of your ravishment so that I can claim you."

"You do, hey? You might want to let me get used to this idea."

"You've got tonight."

"Jeez. Fast engagement." From the mischievous gleam in her eye she wasn't too concerned. She reached up and brushed her fingers over his lips then down his cheekbone to his jaw. A smile bloomed and her next words, though quiet, seemed laced with awe. "He's right. I wish he wasn't, but he is. I love you, Stom."

He could tell she wanted him to say the same, but it was not happening in his head. When he didn't have her in his arms it was so immense a disaster that he shut down. Nothing had mattered but her and owning her again. Now, with her heart beating against his chest and the subtle fragrance of her body calming him, other thoughts had swirled in and made a quagmire. Love was bobbing up and down and in danger of sinking.

He was a warrior, and he couldn't be that anymore – couldn't go to battles, couldn't do what he was trained to do. He was shackled to her as much as she was to him. It was not supposed to turn out *this* way. Being told what to do was abhorrent, even if it were his own body doing the commanding.

To give himself time, he readjusted his hold on her, smiling though at the softness of her breast under his hand and the shift of her curls across his shoulder.

"That word…it's hard for me to say so soon. I'm sure I can't live without you, Willow." He kissed her fingers and studied this female who had reached somewhere inside him that had long ago become a deserted, lonely place. "But it's too fast a change for me to wrap my tongue and my head around that 'love' word. I have a desire to collar you again and attach a leash so I can yank on it if you try to get away. And if someone tries to take you from me, I will nail them to a door with a whole set of knives and forks, possibly even spoons. Will that satisfy you for now?"

"Spoons?" She snorted and her mouth crimped up at the corners. "If you weren't around, I'd be checking to see if the sun had fallen out of the sky. But I can hope you will say it? Like it's just around the corner?"

She deserved honesty. "Probably."

"Okay. Fine. It's pathetic and all but I can wait a few million years for you to say it."

"Good."

There was, he decided, a line between love and this gnawing stark compulsion to possess her. No matter what Dassenze had said, what existed here trod on new ground. He wasn't giving her up anyway. But love? Love was something he needed to grow into. *Mine*, however, that could be instant and he'd stamped it on her with the mark she now wore.

"So. Where is this ravishment happening? On this planet, your god said. London? Paris?"

"Ahh. No. Somewhere closer. Your house seems the safest. Tomorrow morning. Don't bother wearing underwear."

"My house? Are you sleeping in my bed tonight?"

"Yes."

"Mmm. Good." Willow turned her face into his chest and inhaled. "I'll let Ally go to that appointment. She'll be safe at the hospital. We can be alone and you can be as bad as you want."

"Bad? You don't know the meaning of that word." The things he might do to her.

"One thing. You have to tell me what happens to Ally after this. I don't know what to do." She clamped her eyes shut. "I can't leave her but I can't leave you. It's like I'm some sort of magnetized ball bouncing from one to the other. Makes my head hurt."

"I will. I'll think it through. We can talk. I'll get some answers from Dassenze as soon as we can manage it. Though that could take days. Trust me. If I do anything, I do it right."

"Days? I guess…"

Three Preyfinders emerged from beneath the trees and Brask snapped orders at them. They bore off-world equipment. The mess here would need more than merely picking up the pieces.

When Willow snuggled into him some more, he grinned down at her, then started walking.

"You know you're naked, Stom?"

"Yes. That was Dassenze's doing. I had to be for the cocoon to work." And other things he was never mentioning to her.

"Okay. Just, you're going to scare the locals, and maybe some koalas are going to need therapy."

"They'll get over it."

His one regret – forgetting to ask Dassenze about Ally. Could he claim her too in some non-sexual way? Or was there some other way?

Chapter 18

Whatever had Dassenze meant? Brask examined Talia. The Ascend had already taken a few women as his pets. But this one, Talia? His words had been ambiguous, as if he knew what Brask was imagining. That was possible. No one seemed sure of all a god's powers.

"*This one is too wild for just you.*"

The *just* made him wonder. Did a god ever share? And, he'd almost seemed to give permission.

The idea made him decide on that something he'd thought of earlier.

She was still unconscious, by virtue of a few extra *looks* he'd used. He checked and saw the last of his men nod to him and head for their vehicles. The place was clear, except for him, and her, this woman who could track him from across a continent.

In his pocket was the sample of pet nano-chem. He reached in and snapped off the lid, tipped it up and allowed the smallest smear to wet his finger. Then he knelt beside her.

Such a stunning woman. That first time he'd seen her, in the midst of devastation, she'd taken his breath away. Lithe, determined, a fighting Earth woman with a sword, and today, she'd been so fast the air had hummed. Every time he looked in her eyes, he saw a new variant of blue.

Rules weren't made to be broken, yet he was about to break one of the biggest rules ever.

"Pretty thing," he murmured, nudging aside her lips and moving his finger a half inch inside. "Want to be mine?"

Kissing her might be the preferred delivery method – assuming you didn't fuck them – but somehow, this way made the air sizzle with eroticism.

He felt the wetness as the tip of her tongue moved against his skin. "That's it." Then, when she truly sucked on his finger, just that once, he couldn't help growling with triumph.

Just one thing to remember, don't fall in love like Stom. That part was easy, though. He had a heart of stone.

*****

When they returned, Ally eased herself out of the cave of shrubs and brushed away the bits of leaves that had tangled in her dress. She shucked off the aura of concealment and climbed up the embankment. *People* and all their messy emotions rushed into her head and she had to struggle to control it. The ache thumped about like a monster stomping through her mind. Then she clamped down again. This close to the house she could do it easily.

After all these years and years of practice, though she wasn't sure why or how it worked, the house was a shelter that let her not hear all the trillions and billions of bad thoughts that people had every day of their lives. Peace reigned.

"Hi!" She waved and ran up to them.

Stom was naked but that didn't bother her. As a rule, men did little for her. A few had made her stop and stare out the window, tears silently rolling down her face. That had been in her teenage years, mostly, knowing that the boy wasn't for her, the sad girl locked away in her self-imposed cage.

She had tried to go out, back then, only to be left clinging to her sanity by her fingernails. Those few times, her worst destiny had called to her and left her dangling above a vast chasm seething with the screams of the lost. She'd woken in hospital. Drugged. Numb. Her mind like blotting paper.

It was best to stay in the house, to curl herself in a ball and show only her spikes to those who meant her harm.

Stom was out of bounds anyway. He and Ally resonated, like a note ringing in perfect tune. He had a nice mind, different, kind, and he didn't mess up her head like most. She ran ahead of them to open the back door while Stom put Willow on her feet.

Something happened in the forest.

"You're okay, Ally?" Willow asked, as if striving to keep the tears from her voice. She reached out and squeezed Ally's hand.

"Sure. Course I am." Then she gave Willow a little kiss on the cheek. "Come on in. I'll make some tea." She gave Stom a hesitant look. Maybe he was good but she'd learned that everyone had their own agenda. "Are you going to keep Willow and me safe now?"

"I am."

Long ago, she'd learned to tighten down her focus, but as far as she could detect, he was sincere.

"Good."

What had happened out there? Something dreadful had trailed its foulness over her cousin. From Stom, she caught a whisper, a suggestion, of how close she had come to a terrible end. She wished she could protect Willow out there the same as Willow tried to protect her. Hobbled, lame, useless, that was her. Only here in the house was she any good, because this was her kingdom.

Lately there'd been so many weird half-people *things* out there that hiding in the culvert had been dicey.

"*You* are not coming in," she said to the outdoors before closing the door.

Chapter 19

Willow waved as the taxi did a U-turn and drove off. Ally's ashen face with the downturned mouth was all she could see for many yards until the taxi was blocked by other cars merging into the traffic.

It's nothing. She'll be fine.

She sat on the porch as Stom had requested, waiting. Some Preyfinders had pulled up in a black Jeep with darkened windows. Carrying large overstuffed bags, they filed past the house down the side and she heard Stom let them in the back door. Whatever they were doing, it was a secret. She sighed. Considering how important today was, she'd hoped they could keep battle negotiations or discussing what to wear at the next Preyfinder ball for another time.

The day had started badly, perhaps that meant it would end well?

Getting Ally to go in the subsidized taxi to hospital appointments had often been a major expedition, so she'd reinforced the medications this morning by using the extra dose. The doctors said it was okay as a once-in-a-blue-moon thing. The driver knew not to take her anywhere except to the clinic, and staff would meet her at the door. Why did this always feel like feeding a guppy to an aquarium of moray eels? It was for the best today, though; she was such an innocent. Stom's plans would likely turn Ally's brain inside out if she was in the house.

The compulsion was there and made her doubt herself. Sometimes she wanted to please him too much. Was she a laboratory mouse bumping and bumping the dispenser button to get more food?

She sighed then let a smile grow as anticipation wriggled its way to the front of her thoughts and bounced up and down.

After today, she would be *his*. An outcome that, logically, she would've been appalled by a few days ago, yet now she wanted dearly. Without him she would die – literally. Her damn heart would stop. The shaking, blacking out, and throwing up had better not manifest when he went down the road for a carton of milk.

She hugged her knees. Life with Stom had a big potential for hurt, and she didn't care a single jot. There was something *more* about life with him. An impossible yet seriously infinite spice was added.

But… *Oh my, Stom.*

"Would I have loved you if this pet nano-chem hadn't been used on me?" *Shit.* What a dumb question, but it dug its claws into her and wouldn't leave.

She rocked her chin on her hands for a moment. Yes? She remembered all that she'd seen of him, knew of him. Even this devotion to his dead family reeked of a stupidly loyal, good man. She would have fallen for him anyway, once she got over the alien crap, in about ten years' time.

Love plus this nano-chem, all it had done was make possible something that otherwise would've had her screaming and running.

The Preyfinders left, none of them sparing her a glance. Cheerful lot.

What happened after today wasn't just to do with her. Stom had promised to help Ally. What if she could be cured of this mental illness that made her shy away from other people and the outdoors? That would justify almost anything. This one day of sacrifice was a whisper in the wind compared to the vision of Ally running screaming with joy down a street of people, shaking their hands, grabbing kids and hugging and kissing them… Whoah. Okay, that might get her arrested, but still.

She stood and went to the front door. Stom had promised, and she believed in him.

When she closed the door and turned, he was there. Hands behind his back, in a cream shirt and dark brown pants – like a normal handsome man, if you discounted all the black stripes meandering across his skin. His black hair was tousled and she longed to comb it with her fingers, but not to tame it, just to play with it and watch his face while she did so.

A Preyfinder had knocked at the door last night and piled his clothes, his weapons, and the long black coat into her arms. An armored coat, Stom had once told her. She'd gone to her knees with the weight of the damned thing.

She looked coyly at him and turned around slowly with the hem of her little white dress in one hand, lifted just enough to show a hint of her ass. No panties, of course.

"Would Sir like to sample the merchandise?"

He beckoned with one finger and revealed that in his other hand he held the leash he'd used on her in the forest. But in the hand doing the beckoning, something flashed in the light.

"I have a gift for you."

"Jewelry?"

"Could be. Come here so I can show you what a good Feya pet wears."

"I thought I was a mate and not a pet?" She danced a little closer, thinking of holding back and teasing, but his reach was longer than she suspected. Stom grabbed her arm and brought her in.

"Stand there. You're whatever I say you are since your mark is still maturing. See how the color is filling in?"

Feather light, he ran his finger around the twisted red spiral on her left upper arm then he tucked that finger under the shoestring strap of the dress.

"What a pretty pet, you are." As he spoke, he ran his finger up and down under the strap, reminding her how close he was to the upper swell of her breast. Then he smiled that gorgeous yet deviant smile that said to her: *I know you're turned on and I plan to molest you soon.*

Her tongue came out all on its own to touch her upper lip.

When his eyes narrowed, she zipped it back into her mouth.

"A pet, legally, has few rights before her Master. I plan to test out my pet properly today. Before she turns into my mate."

The promise in that gave her pause. No rights? Scary, yet intriguing. In his unique fashion, Stom was the epitome of a good bad man.

"Mm. I think I can handle that." When she went to sneak up on her toes to kiss him, he pushed down on her shoulders.

"Stay. Or I might get ideas. I have yet to show you how I punish my pet girl."

The minor threat was enough to make her feel that familiar heated tingle below. "How?"

He chuckled then said softly, "You're not supposed to look eager. I need to see something before I show you the jewelry."

With the tips of his fingers, he drew the shoestring straps off her shoulders. Red gemstones glinted and the gold links trailed from his hands across her skin, cold on her upper breasts. Earrings?

Below the bodice of her dress was a little line of elastic, which helped to emphasize her bosom. It also kept the dress from falling to her ankles as he slowly pulled it down to reveal the swell of her breasts. Since she'd not worn a bra or panties, her nipples had been poking at the material since he'd begun with the slave girl threats. Now, they were bare.

And red. Her nipples were extremely red. That surprise was going to take a while to lessen. It made her want to look in the mirror at herself and marvel.

More than even the spiral on her arm, this color seemed to say, *I'm His*.

Expressionless, Stom lifted her breasts and caressed them with his thumb, encouraging her nipples to bunch even tighter. She sucked in a breath, savoring the feeling, parting her mouth as the sensations grew and sent out erotic signals. When he touched them too roughly, she wriggled and scrunched her toes. Today, they were excruciatingly sensitive. The bonding, perhaps?

"On a pet, these need decoration." With finger and thumb, he firmly trapped both her nipples.

She tried not to look too worried but her lower lip curled down. "They do?"

"Mm-hm. Yes, they do."

She recognized the jewelry as nipple clamps – having seen something similar on a website she'd browsed. "Kinky. I know what those are."

"Do you? I suppose when females have nipples there are only so many things one can do with them. Though for Feya, this is a tradition on obtaining a pet."

"You decorate them?"

"We do. Wherever our color shows." There was a glint in his eye that made her think fast.

"My…" The lips of her pussy were red. Her cheeks warmed. "Not there!"

"No?" His voice dropped into a gravely tone that sent a delicious quake through her. "Does my pet think to refuse?"

"Umm. I guess, maybe, not?" She twisted up one brow, not wanting to disappoint him. The idea of him doing this had her imagining the feel of his hands and him making her sit still while he found her clit. She stumbled to ask the obvious. "Will it hurt much?"

Stom chuckled. "You'll find out soon."

Instead of applying the clamps, he released her.

"First this." He took the red collar from his pocket and locked that onto her neck, firm, yet careful.

He'd not even asked if he could do that, and at the hypnotizing stroke of his finger on her neck, tracing above the collar, she shivered, her eyelids lowering as she savored the sensation.

"Does my pet like that?"

The words sank in but she kept her eyes down.

"Willow?"

She heaved in a breath, slow as the ocean. "Yes."

Then, as reverent as an artist putting the final touches on a sculpture, he went to one knee and drew her dress the rest of the way down, wiggling it over the curves of her ass then past her upper thighs. He held her hip and helped her step from the pool of cloth at her feet.

She stood naked before him.

"Now this," he said as he smoothed his palm up her thigh, "This is you, only you."

With his mouth so close to the *vee* at the top of her legs she felt paralyzed, ready to obey whatever orders he might give her. But he only rested the side of his face on her belly and wrapped his arms about her lower body. For a while he said and did nothing more. Puzzled, she threaded her hand into his hair, enjoying the feel of it running across her fingers.

"Are you okay?"

He stroked her ass then cupped one side with the whole of his large hand. "Shh. Yes. Yes, I am. I'm appreciating you. You smell so good, feel so good." Then he turned his head and nipped above her hip. She jumped.

"Ow!"

"You interrupted my meditation."

Since he couldn't see, she stuck her tongue out but then had to suppress a giggle. This was Stom being a little sillier than his usual self. She let him be, breathing quietly, enjoying touching him and him touching her. Standing here naked with Stom doing this made her feel like she was on the edge of something, about to step off into space, but with him by her side it was safe. She could do anything if he was there too.

In the forest, he'd said he wasn't in love. Yet hope was rising.

He rose to his feet and took her hand. "Come."

Then he led her to her bedroom, with the hallway rug soft under her bare feet, and he let her enter the room first, his palm at the small of her back.

The scent of tangy tree sap and flower blossom made her aware that something was different even before she registered what was before her. She padded in. Stom followed and waited behind her, resting his hands on her waist.

"Wow. What have you been doing?"

Her bed was still her bed, though covered by a cloth embellished in some alien yet vaguely Arabian theme. On her normally staid bed, the cloth was an invasion of vibrant metallic shades of pink, blue and green. The edges of her room had been made a forest. Tree limbs crisscrossed with drooping branches and foliage. If her other furniture was here, it was lost behind the leaves. Even the ceiling was barely visible, with fresh branches weaving together as if they'd grown there. The recessed lights cast dappled shadows that swayed and shifted.

She took another step. Petals of rose and daisy were strewn across the bed cloth, and the air wept the scent of crushed flowers. It woke her soul.

She inhaled, half closing her eyes, and held out her hands, palm upward as if to catch rain that was about to fall. The fragrance alone made her imagine she was in the midst of some far away jungle.

"Stom," she turned in his arms, smiling shyly, "this is beautiful and incredible and –"

"Shh." He enfolded her until his arms caged her, gentle, though the muscles of his biceps were hard as stone. When he kissed her, their lips met in a sweet and soft caress.

Then he undressed and drew her forward until he could sit on the bed with her standing before him.

"Be good for me." This time each of his kisses met her nipples. He sucked on each a few times, enough to make her gasp, and his teeth followed through with light tug.

Her throat tightened. "That's hot." When he approached her nipple with the little clamps, she wanted to duck backward but she made herself be still. The gems swung at the end of the clamp. The jaws enclosed her nipple.

Not good! Not good! Her belly tensed and she couldn't help a whine escaping.

"Be still," Stom muttered as he screwed the clamp tighter. He kissed the underside of her breast. "These are so pretty on you. I only need them to stay on. I don't need pain from you."

"Can I put some on you then?" Her challenge resulted in him giving the dangling metal a tug. "Owie. I guess that's a no. It is hurting. Umm. Or maybe not."

The pain pulsed, excruciating one second, then somehow it flipped and pleasure returned, expanding as blood coursed through the nipple.

It hurt, but not impossibly so, and she loved seeing him do it to her, knowing he'd put each clamp on her. She loved the pleasure he took from this. When he placed the second one, she only squirmed a little.

"Much prettier than one." He tapped each gem-stoned weight, sending them swinging.

Her femaleness seemed emphasized, her breasts on display and heavier. When he stroked her, she hummed and met his gaze. *More.*

"I'm glad you like them. Now, open your legs." He shifted back on the bed and showed her the last clamp. "This one is merely for decoration, Willow."

Though not convinced, she shuffled closer. There was a darkness to Stom's gaze which almost made her fear. With one hand on her ass, he urged her between his legs. His other hand separated her thighs, exposing her intimately. He inspected her.

"I need to do some encouraging. It's not coming out to play."

"It?" she whispered, blushing. "*It* is sensible."

"But until it comes out, I can't make you mine. I just need it begging me. Out where I can see it."

He looked up at her, and winked, then he lowered his head and dabbed at her clit with his tongue. The flutter that shot through her made her jerk, then go *mmm* in appreciation, especially since he drew his finger along her seam, gathered her moisture, and wiggled that finger up inside.

He kept his tongue busy, working in closer, sucking on the tiny nub to make it engorge, and she couldn't help watching, enthralled.

His mouth on her…especially when he put it over her pussy like he was going to swallow her entirely. *Man.* She clutched the back of his head with both hands, grinding on him gently.

He pulled away and wiped his mouth. The clamp reappeared in his hand.

"I love your mouth on me there," she ventured, pouting. She circled her hips, hoping to distract him, hoping to delay.

"And I would love to see you come as I eat your pussy, but I want you to sit on me. Today, I want to watch your eyes as you come while I'm inside you. And first, we need this." He dangled it high.

Determined man. But it was part of his ritual. She sucked on her lip a moment, eyeing the clamp and scowling. Then she sighed and sidled forward. She pushed out her mons, frowning as he *V'd* his fingers, isolated her clit, and stretched aside her lips. Even she could see that her clit was more engorged. The things he'd done with his tongue. She needed more of that.

When the clamp approached, she flinched.

He grinned at her reluctance. "This goes on the less sensitive part of you. My human anatomy lesson says you have that."

"I won't look." She covered her eyes with both hands.

Once more, he pushed her thighs apart, then she felt him pinch a part of her clit, and hard metal slid around it. By then she was examining the ceiling. Tree bits, tree bits…he's not about to – *eep*.

The pain was small and ratcheted up for a moment then he freed her.

With his hands on the back of her thighs, Stom kept her legs still. He studied her clit and its decoration. Her wetness shone on his fingers and he ran a finger along her cleft, until he found and nudged at her entrance.

"Now you look like my pet."

When he reapplied his mouth to her, the suction threw her back into that recent body memory. Orgasm approaching rapidly. *Damn*. But pain niggled, held her back. The bite on her nipples, the small tight sting on her clit. Too much input. Defying the pain, the heat of pleasure built. The craving swelled. The slide of his fingers in her wetness then curving up inside her, forcing apart her walls, sent her arching, groaning.

While his tongue flicked on her, he slipped a third finger inside. His thumb played near her clit, around and around, stretching her, wet with her juices and his mouth. His hands held her still for his wicked, wicked tongue.

"I can't. I can't —" She panted, squealed, hands clawing into his hard muscled back. When she looked down, frantic, she saw red scratch marks on his skin.

More slippery licks encircled her clit, close to where the clamp held her fast in its jaws.

Her pussy clenched onto his three fingers and she screamed a little, digging her fingers into his muscled shoulders, as if he were the only life raft in the face of a tsunami. She shuddered into an unrelenting orgasm. The echoes ran on until she at last collapsed, exhausted, onto his shoulder.

"*Can't* seems to mean *can* for you."

Sarcasm?

Still catching her breath, through half-lidded eyes she looked down at him. The man was as smug as could be. His erect cock poked up between his thighs, clearly begging her.

She toyed with her lip. "Can I have you in me? Please?"

"Up." He slapped her ass once and encouraged her to stand properly. Then he hoisted her onto his thighs with her legs spread as wide as they could go. His cock, she felt it poke her there, slipping, an inch away from nirvana. She so loved the feel of a man's cock going in after a climax.

"Push yourself onto me." He held her gaze, unblinking. "Don't look away."

With his hands guiding her, she lowered herself until the tip of his cock slowly entered her. Blunt, with that softness over the hard, sliding, her moisture lubricating the glide. Inexorable.

"Ohh." She arched her head back, thrust out her breasts, and wriggled. She'd looked away.

Yet he only cradled her, supporting her as she leaned back, grabbing a handful of hair so she had to arch a little more. "Keep going."

"Am." She grunted.

An orgasm only made her hunger to be filled. His cock widened her, pushing in, further, ever inward. She sat lower and lower, feeling every amazing inch of him.

"When we are done. Your arm will be fully red."

He gave details? Now? She tried to reply but he'd fully penetrated her, and her butt rested on his legs. Nothing else mattered. With that mesmerizing her, language wasn't happening. Her eyes rolled up and her intended words came out as a breathy moan.

Her moan turned into a sharp intake as Stom used his brutal grip on her body to withdraw then thrust upward. The nipple clamps and the one on her clit jerked and wobbled, which made her gasp yet again.

His hand found each clamp and tugged on them while he built a rhythm of small thrusts, slapping against her ass and thighs.

An orgasm hit her, rumbling through, flattening her mind for a few precious seconds. When she opened her eyes, she found him watching.

He kissed the hollow at the base of her neck. "I could do this a hundred thousand times and never grow tired of seeing your face."

She mumbled and tried to cuddle.

"Not yet." His eyes were bright.

Though she whimpered a protest, he stood suddenly, and arranged her so she was on hands and knees on the bed. The clamps swung merrily.

"I should've made these bells," he growled, giving the clit one a tweak before he mounted her from behind.

His cock sliding in... *Fuck.*

The slam of him against her butt made her decorations swing some more. The weights jerked. She sucked in a groan, reveling in the tugging at her nipples and clit, feeling exquisitely female, wanted, and fucked.

Sensations multiplied as Stom put his hand to her pussy and rubbed her clit, rotating his finger. She bowed her spine, presenting herself for even easier access to her man. His thrusts grew more violent, the last few positively rough and vicious. She squealed, clamping onto his cock, tight. The swell of his cum far up inside her triggered another mini-climax.

His hot breath on her ear, made her smile in satisfaction. She blinked away sweat, happy to wait a while, with his weight on her and his chin on her neck. After one kiss, he pulled her onto his lap and petted her.

"Am I changed?" she whispered, searching his eyes, amazed that she finally had this man to herself.

"Almost. Not quite. I think I need to fuck you again so we can get the last bit shaded."

"What?" She peeked. Her arm was all red in a dark red spiral. "Liar."

"For that," he bit the side of her neck, snarling making her squeal again, "For that I get to tie you up too. Defying me is punishable by tying up and fucking."

"Perhaps I should defy you more often," she mumbled into his chest.

"Devil girl." He squeezed her and laughed. "Before I do that. I plan to look at you while we eat some of the delicacies they brought me. And drink some of the finest Feya wine the Preyfinders could find here. Which means a Chablis, strawberries, and cheese from Australia, and some chocolates from Sweden."

Willow guffawed. "I wondered."

"I'll take these off now, but keep them for those special times when I need a pet." Stom stroked the side of her nipple, and smiled. "I might have a lot of those times."

"Mmm." Disagreeing with that was not happening.

Then he removed all the clamps, kissing her gently on the sore places when she flinched. With her hands resting on his shoulders, she watched him. A quiet sense of both awe and wonder cloaked this moment. How had she ever gotten this lucky?

When she pottered back from the kitchen with the platter of food and the wine, she found Stom answering some Preyfinder message that only he could hear. He nodded and said something like, they'd be fine, and that if they really needed him, he was available.

"Nothing," he said to her, dismissing the message. "They don't need me."

Good. This day should be theirs to cherish.

Sitting on the bed with Stom, naked, drinking ice cold Chablis from a goblet at ten in the morning was so different from what she'd expected from her life. Tears trickled down her face. She sniffed.

"I hope those are happy tears?" When he pulled her into his side, she shrugged but let him study her and track the tears with his forefinger.

"They are." She smiled, her mouth twisting. "I always thought I'd be forever with Ally, alone, trying to sort out life by myself. She isn't a lot of help on some days."

"And this is better?" he asked softly.

"Oh yes. Much. Now I have you."

When she looked up shyly he bent and kissed her, a sweet, almost chaste kiss. Not sexual passion, but a simple kiss that spoke of, perhaps, the love he'd not yet mentioned.

Then he held her for a long time. The silence between them was an easy one, as if they'd known each other for many years.

This man surrounded her, warm, secure, keeping the bad out, being her barricade and her shield. He would be her friend too in time, she was sure. This was a reality so good, so solid, and so fucking incredible, that it made her afraid to rise. Absentmindedly, she manipulated his fingers and ran her hand back and forth along the muscles of his forearm. She had a weird urge to stay here with him on the bed, feeling that if she parted from him this might shatter.

There was evil in the world and she could bear the possibility of it leaping on her when the alternative was the weary life she'd borne until this moment. Now she'd found a man she could love until her last breath and fear nibbled at her.

Silly, but true.

"I used to think the same, Willow. I thought I'd die alone on a strange planet. I think even my bones were teeming with hate for the enemy. I would've bitten my way through a horde of them if my last weapon was gone and I only had teeth. I hated so much."

"What is this?" He traced the ugly scar on her forearm. "Something to do with Ally?"

"No. No, not at all. It's from when I was a kid. A burn scar." Of all the things for him to notice.

"Yes? You were hurt badly?"

She shook her head. "No. My parents though, they died. It was a house fire." She couldn't *not* tell him this, though it hurt. "I've often wondered if I caused it. People said I had a habit of messing with matches, lighters." She gnawed on her bottom lip.

"That's only a bad memory. You were a child. It was a terrible thing, but you must get over it. It's the past." His swallow and silence made it clear some thought had impinged. "Like my own past."

"Yours is more recent. I told you, I have time. I can wait for you to believe you love me. *I* love you. That's enough for now."

"Thank you." He stroked her hair.

She nestled in. Both of them had ugliness in the past, but hers, she'd gotten over it, mostly. It seemed as if he were on the verge of saying he loved her too, but even if he never did say those words, it didn't matter because she knew he did.

"I'm happy, Stom."

He sighed then slid off the bed.

Carefully he took away both their goblets and the food and set them aside. "I too am happy, because…" He grinned and wrapped his hands over her ankles where she had her legs stretched before her. "Because I can do this."

He yanked her legs forward and climbed on top of her as she squealed. The leash, a scarf or two, and a belt, made quick bondage and he rendered her helpless then sat on her. From the lightness he was trying not to squash her.

"Now, what can I do with you?"

She giggled. "I can see you twirling your moustache like some evil villain."

"A moustache? I will have to look that one up. Not in my language base."

That was when the world exploded.

Glass shattered and tinkled and objects, black and tumbling, arrived in the room, flying across. Bottles? The utter shock of the next explosion rocked the house, and scattered all the tree bits and pieces into a whirling ember-filled maelstrom. Everything burned.

Even Stom. The force had thrown him up and off the bed. The temperature in the room had peaked quickly with the ignition of some volatile liquid. The room was wrenched into the worst possible state of fire and he became a man on fire in an instant. Her lungs strained for air. Instead she gulped down fire.

The house? Why had the house failed them?

Stom stood and struggled to walk to her but fell.

Aghast, she saw the flames eat at him, turning him black, turning him into a man-sized shape of sizzling charcoal and destroyed skin and muscle. And she lay there on the bed, screaming, writhing, tormented, as everything burned. The ropes burned, the scarves, the belt.

Her arms tore forward as one scarf snapped. Her legs bonds ripped. She was free.

Into the torrent of the rippling monster, the roaring orange-and-black foe, she stalked. The fire played on her bones and eyes, toying, making her die a thousand times over from the wretched agonies, but she made it to him, there on the floor, the hunched-over thing, and she dragged his coat to him and herself and she hugged him. To keep him safe. Like she'd tried with her parents.

She'd failed, yet again. His skin was making bubbling and crackling noises under her ear. He breathed in rasping lung-tearing groans but he was dead and she knew it. Nothing and no one could survive in this. Except her. She burned and yet she did not. The fire licked at her, dazzled her with pain, yet beneath it she could see her pinkness and the tiny hairs on her arm swaying as if in a breeze.

Now she knew how ugly life was; it had brought him to her as her salvation then torn him away from her. It had shown her what she was.

When they came, striding through the still-hungry fires in their suits and masks, she fought them, but they took her away from her love. She wanted to save him and couldn't.

Ally appeared in the smoking, fire-wreathed doorway then turned to run but they caught her too. Of all the days for her to escape her minders… Willow watched, trapped in the enemy's grasp. These men had killed so effortlessly. The tears in her eyes never shed. She was past crying, past devastation, gone into the land of the anesthetized and silent.

She didn't know how it was that she could walk through such a fire and live, and she didn't care. Evil had found her again. Perhaps it always did when she was happy.

Chapter 20

The alert came as Brask shot down the last of the Bak-lal. He holstered the HK at his back, ignoring the urgent beep in his ear comm for a few seconds as he scanned for life. The countdown ticker said they'd got all the suspects – difficult to find these until they showed up by doing something out of character for normal humans. These were no soldiers, not modified for war – simply people with some Bak-lal mind alterations. Mean motherfuckers in Earth lingo.

But the lack of armaments and hard-wired nerves meant the Preyfinder AI couldn't find them easily in the data stream.

These had emerged from hiding and killed along with the Bak-lal at two other locations. He'd had to commit almost every man on this island continent to maintain control. Why? There must be a reason.

They'd fought desperately, intending to kill by any means possible, but with only human guns and knives in their hands. The underground car park stank of smoke and blood and cordite from the guns. His men were hauling bodies, some in fragments.

Perhaps this was best. A full guts and glory battle with Bak-lal with no god available to back up the Preyfinders' actions might mean irretrievable exposure to humans.

The message was from the operations coordinator at the ship.

"Guard me," he signaled to his second in command, Jadd.

Prompted by the message title, he flicked on the holo, and was confronted by a house consumed by fire. The flames leapt thirty feet in the air and the building was surrounded by units from the fire brigade, police, and ambulance.

That house, he knew it. His stomach wrenched.

"Where is this?" he barked.

"The house owned by Willow," said the coordinator. "Both Stom and her were known to be there. We've only just restored drone coverage, sir. Our orbiting drone was incapacitated by a Bak-lal strike. Where it came from, we don't know as yet."

All this information said that this, where he stood, was a diversion. Had the Bak-lal wanted Stom?

"Did you retrieve Stom? Or anyone?" That inferno looked survivable, if he'd been wearing his coat. If not… He clamped down on his emotional response.

"The humans have him. I'm tracking the ambulance. Seven minutes to arrival at the hospital. From drone images, he's dying." A picture flashed up: a black man-shaped thing on a stretcher being covered by a silvery cloth. "No one else was brought out. We had no units, no men except the core defense manning the ship, sir. Permission to use those to retrieve Stom?"

Even the operator sounded stressed. Stom's chances of surviving were tiny, but they had to retrieve him. Brask pressed his knuckles into his forehead. Risk exposure by mounting an operation on a moving ambulance? Risk depriving the ship of its core personnel?

One of the other strike teams was closer than his.

"Accor? How fast can he get there compared to a team from the ship?"

"They can make it. Estimated one-minute difference. His team is returning here already."

"Good." He drew in a long breath and committed. "I authorize a non-lethal strike on the ambulance by Accor's team. I also authorize the use of a ship's shuttle to return him to the ship. Make sure everything is standing by. Alert medical personnel."

"Sir."

He snapped off the holo and swiveled on one heel. "Jadd. You're in charge."

At a jog, he headed for the nearest transport. With no god, their ability to manipulate all the many human means of recording and exchanging information was small. This was out in the open, on a street, in daylight. All it would take when the team hit the ambulance was one man they didn't spot recording a video and uploading it to YouTube.

His career might be heading down the toilet but for once he didn't care. He'd thrown away enough potential friends over the years. Stom was a man he'd grown to like.

When he reached the ship, Stom was already assessed, hooked up to resuscitators and regenerators, and from the tubes and humming gadgets, the docs had plugged him into everything the ship possessed. Possibly including even the games machine from level three.

Brask stopped and stared at the organized chaos. Medical personnel were rattling about, extracting fluids, doing a kakload of stuff to Stom, who was entirely hidden under a half-cylindrical white machine. He sneaked in to question the least busy one, who was playing with data on a screen.

He jerked his chin toward Stom. "How's he going? I can see you've got a lot to do –"

The man glanced up and grimaced. "Sir, honestly, he's going to die. Most of him is cooked so deep I don't know how he's still alive. He's in no pain. We have him anesthetized, but he is going to die. You can't regen charcoal."

Stunned was the best word. He couldn't move, couldn't mouth a single syllable for several seconds.

Do your job. The man looked white. They hadn't had a death here for months.

He reached out and patted the man's shoulder. "You did good, Terek. Thank you."

His reply sounded as if it came from a tunnel a thousand yards long and Brask barely processed the meaning.

A message beep. He answered it.

"Sir. From cobbled together, retrieved human footage, we've found at least one vehicle leaving the area of the house with Willow inside. She doesn't appear injured though she was naked. AI analysis says at least one of her captors is Bak-lal. The other woman, Ally, has gone missing also. She's probably been captured by whoever has Willow."

"Good." He nodded. Getting somewhere. "Where is this vehicle? Where are the women?"

"We don't know, Sir. They were headed north but that's no guarantee as to destination."

"Fuck." She wasn't injured. In that blaze? Stom would not have sat still to be burned. It had to be a surprise attack and that meant she would have been there too, surely. Not injured? What was going on here? Another woman of power? That conclusion was a stretch of logic.

He wished Dassenze was here.

"Put every priority on finding those women." The Bak-lal queen, wherever she was, had come out of hiding for them. She'd thrown away resources, revealed her hand. What had seemed a curious ability must have far more significance. If Stom had to die, at least let him get revenge for this. They would find this queen. They would kill it.

Chapter 21

Though she'd figured her situation could get no worse, when they dragged Ally past her door, Willow felt something crumble inside, and she wept.

Wherever this place was, it was near a town. The distant roar of traffic reached her now and then. They'd tied her up with steel handcuffs, left her on the bed, and used the collar Stom had given her to attach her to the headboard. That corruption of something he'd gifted to her had hurt. Yet another fresh, heart-deep wound to add to the general mutilation.

He was gone. Nothing could survive that fire. Except her, it seemed. The stench of the smoke permeated her hair and soot covered her skin, coated the insides of her mouth. She'd breathed fire, walked in it, and she lived, unscathed.

The ache within was enough to keep her head going round and round, reliving the agony of seeing him burn. But she'd held herself together. She'd held in the tears, she had, until Ally appeared.

Now sweet, innocent Ally was here too. She expected herself to be raped and killed at any moment. That she could stand. People who could do what she'd seen and not flinch, who had laughed in the car as they drove away, those people might do anything.

But Ally was here. *Fuck.*

She cried despairing tears for the girl in another room who knew so little of what horrors the world could visit upon her. She'd always stopped harm from reaching her. Was she going to fail at that too?

This terrible fact stirred a need in her. It drove past the sorrow and the horror, kicked away the crutch of self-destruction. It made her start to think again.

I have to get out, somehow. Have to take her with me.

She sat up, wiped away the tears with her handcuffed wrist, and she thought. Forget the men in the next room, the dead place in her chest.

The fire.

Forget.

Methodical, she should be methodical. She went through a list. What was in the room? Could she use anything to escape? Who had she seen? How many? What could she hear them say? Her list went on forever.

Things happened around her. Strange thuds and clanks. Voices.

The screams from some anonymous woman in a nearby room were chilling, especially when men laughed again, not Ally though, thank god, but this time the sounds didn't shut her down or stop her thinking. She wouldn't give in anymore. Now she had a goal.

She listened to the screams grow quieter as perhaps the woman weakened then she fell silent.

In what sort of neighborhood would a woman's screams go unnoticed?

A very bad one, said her logical self.

The half-open cupboard across the room held shoes, both men's and women's and there were dresses and shirts. A couple had lived here. Were they dead? Was that her in the next room? This house might have been hers.

Why had *her* house failed after all those years? Had Stom being there somehow interfered? Had he annoyed the ghost or whatever did the guarding? Or had something else changed?

They fed her that day and two men took her out to a toilet. Though one of them sneered, neither sexually assaulted her. When all was quiet that night, she listened closely and recognized the name Kasper in the conversations. Again with the chills. The fear. The shaking. She watched her hands shaking and they no longer seemed her hands. There was a dark terrible fear that made it impossible to sleep until she was so exhausted that her eyes refused to stay open.

In the morning, she asked herself the logical question. *What could he do to me that is worse than watching Stom die?*

Answer: nothing.

That worked.

She had a wall, a concept to use. Except she had to stay alive long enough to get Ally out.

At around noon, they dragged her into a new room where she saw Ally, tied down on a table, but at least they'd let her keep her dress. It was as if most of these men no longer cared about sex. Their eyes were blank. A dead woman occupied another table, her arms and legs taped into a spread-eagled position. Trails of clotted blood led from wounds in her wrists and ankles.

Her steadfast, cast-iron, I-will-not-fear rule shattered into a thousand pieces.

Kasper sat in a single lounge chair watching it all like a king. Only his eyes were wrong. Even for a cold blooded, ice-in-his-veins criminal, his eyes were so wrong. He blinked too slowly and reminded her of a great lizard sunning itself in the heat of the day. Deep inside there, she knew, this was no longer Kasper. Something else moved behind the façade.

"What are you?" He sat forward, his gaze piercing, as if he could question her mind to mind.

"I'm nothing. No one," she whispered, while trying to check out Ally.

Had they dosed her up with something? She drooled from slack lips and focused on the bare wall. An intravenous infusion tube ran from her arm to a bag of fluids.

Swear words rambled through her head. What could she do? Her fingernails dug into her palms.

Being naked in a room of men daunted her. Disturbed her. But not as much as seeing most of them look past her with cold, emotionless eyes.

Stom had been human in his way. These people were more alien than a man from a thousand suns away.

"You're not *nothing*." Even his voice was distorted, as if his throat had been damaged. "We know. We can tell. My queen can tell and has taught us to see. She –" He pointed at the corpse. "Was one of you. A different human. As is this one who kept your house safe. We know." He leaned back. "And when we learn how to change you, we will have your powers."

"Powers? Me?" She laughed, mocking him even as her mind was telling her to shut up.

"You are the one who lives in fire. She was one who controlled insects. This one here, the alive one, is the protector, the one who gives us headaches."

Ally? He meant her? She looked from her frail cousin to the men. They had drugged her because of headaches? Or they thought she gave them headaches. But, why?

Everything fell into place. Of course. Ally had been the one who had kept her safe all those years.

That morning, she had sent her away. She'd sent away the person who made the house safe. Willow bowed her head. She had therefore killed Stom. Vomit threatened to spill into her mouth. She swallowed it down as she felt the terrible blow. The room shuddered.

She hadn't *known*, couldn't have. Couldn't have. But she'd killed him.

What have I done?

This was helping neither of them. She took a ragged breath.

"What do you want from me?" Slowly she straightened, uncurled her fingers.

"Tell us how you do this. Perhaps we will be kind to you or to her. Tell us."

"Us?" She shook her head. "I don't know."

"The data thinks you know. How can you not know? Tell. Your books speak of rituals, of magic words and objects. You are witches. You have books. Rule books. How do you do it?"

"Books? I... Witches? Us? No. No, you have it wrong. I'm no witch."

He tapped his fingers together then turned to the men. "I think we need to show her. The girl won't die from a finger or two missing. Show her." As the men moved in on Ally, he turned back to Willow and smiled. "We have to wait for our soldier to return with the altered nerve chewers. We hope those will succeed. The last ones failed and killed this woman. In the time we wait, you will talk to us. Proceed." He nodded to his men.

What were they doing? Sweat beaded cold on her skin. They meant to take her finger?

"No! No! You can't." Though fear scrabbled at her, she thrust out her hands, fingers spread, imploring. "Take me. Take one of mine." *Oh god.* Her imagination was vivid and she heard the crunch, saw the jaws closing and severing her finger.

"Gag her." He waved the men forward.

"No!" She tried to back away as they seized her. "Please! Mine! Take my finger! Please, don't touch Ally. Please." She choked out a sob.

Two them held her while a third stuffed cloth in her mouth then placed a strip of tape across her lips.

He'd waited, pitiless. "She is right. Take a toe. Witches are known to use their hands. We don't want to hinder her."

She screamed through the gag when the bolt cutters were applied to Ally's little toe, at the snick and Ally wrenching herself upright, flailing and screeching. Tears ran down Willow's face. Snot came from her nose and she coughed as she struggled to breathe. At the blood dribbling from Ally's foot, she collapsed to her knees. White flooded a cold silence through her mind. The room blurred, spun.

When they ungagged her and neither she nor Ally said anything Kasper seemed to find worthwhile, despite her babbling any rubbish she could think of, he lost interest and ordered them both returned to their rooms.

For hours she sat, hugging her knees, listening to Ally whimpering. When she called out to comfort her, a man came in and slapped her until she stopped.

She licked the blood from her mouth.

These men, all of them deserved to die.

As night fell and shadows thickened, she noticed the red spiral on her arm, touched it with her fingertip. Still the same. Swallowing got difficult. Her mark hadn't changed since the day he died.

Hope kindled. Her thoughts grew, and circled the possibility that had just arrived – a bright pinpoint hope smack in the middle of the blackness. Did that mean anything? Stom's mark on his arm had become a denser, darker red after they had mated. The marks seemed to reflect the state of their relationship.

She buried her face in her hands, massaging her scalp with her clawed-in fingers. Maybe when he died hers would take a while to fade? But she wasn't sick. Maybe when your mate died you lost that link to them. She didn't *know*!

Was it worth hoping? Could he be alive? Or did it mean nothing?

Without hope, she was nothing. She hadn't offered her fingers up for Kasper to chop off for nothing. You couldn't run with toes missing. She'd hoped she could stop him mutilating Ally. She'd wanted to spare her pain but also she'd hoped the girl could get away somehow, sometime, and run.

That was hope: the last thread of flesh caught on the nail of life that stopped you falling into the abyss.

She wiped her nose. Yeah, she was going to hope Stom was alive.

In the meantime no one was rescuing them. What could she do? She had no weapon, no hacksaw. All she had was herself. She was the woman who walked through fire. What good would that do her without matches or anything? Besides, if she set fire to this place, Ally would likely burn before she got to her.

A last reflected ray of sunlight flashed on a shoe buckle in the cupboard.

Fire. What if she could make it as well as survive it?

It might be bullshit but it was also another piece of hope. So she lay on the bed most of that night striving to set alight a piece of paper she found on the floor beside of the bed. Sometimes she even imagined it felt hot.

By morning, by dawn's light, she could see the scrap of paper again. Her eyes were dry and gritty. She rotated the scrap with her finger and thumb. White. It was whiter than white.

Fuckitty fuck. Did I really expect that to work?

That particular hope was looking tatty.

Maybe she should, instead, be trying to undo the handcuffs or get the chain loose?

*****

Brask stared into the regen tank that the black thing floated in. Stom. Flecks of burned flesh peeled away while he watched and were sucked up by the filters. Underneath, some of him was pink.

He made sure his words would come out steady.

"Are you sure?"

"Yes." The medic nodded. "His brain is intact because we prioritized saving that but we don't have more than thirty-five percent of him alive. Even with major prosthetics, major off-world hospital care, organ regen, we'd end up with a brain on a stick, basically, and we're struggling. We don't have the equipment here to get him stable."

Brask swallowed, blinked rapidly. "He's still dying?"

"Yes. I'm sorry, sir. Two hours at most."

"Kak." This was not fair.

The door behind him whisked open. His last hope walked in. Jadd and Brittany.

He held up a finger to indicate they should wait.

The medic stepped back "I'll leave you to make your last tribute to the man. I'm sorry we can't save him. I truly am."

"Thank you." The medic had the wrong assumption there, but he said nothing and watched him leave before he turned to Jadd and Brittany.

They were such a pretty couple, young, full of life. For a moment she rested her head on Jadd's arm. Locks of her auburn hair trickled across the sleeve of his shirt and he leaned her way as if to reassure her. What would it be like to have that sort of bond with a woman?

Brask smiled sadly. These females of Earth seemed to suit his men. There was a uniqueness about them.

"Thank you for coming. I have a strange request for you both. Though perhaps you already know."

"I think perhaps we do, sir." Jadd took his mate's hand, cleared his throat. "What do you need of us?"

"Stom is dying. Nothing we have here can save him." He sucked in a breath and prayed this wouldn't sound too crazy to them. "Can Brittany heal? I've seen evidence that suggests that."

"Uhh." Jadd looked at her then when she whispered *yes* he met Brask's eyes. "Yes, she can. But this. This is far beyond anything –"

"Wait. No, it's not." Her grip on Jadd's hand looked tight enough to strangle all the blood from it but the man merely nodded, encouraging her. "I've healed a man who almost died once before. An enemy. A Bak-lal. The one who I killed at my apartment. Jadd and I figured it out afterward but we've been afraid to say."

"Okay." That she was brave enough to tell him raised her up in his estimation. "I'm glad you're both being honest. Dassenze already suspects this so don't think we're about to persecute you." He looked at them from under his brow. "The evidence suggests there was a widespread burst of life that day, around your apartment. We have nothing to lose. I want you to do whatever it is you do, and try to save him."

"I can try, yes."

The downcast and miserable look didn't tie in with what he expected. "What?"

"Just…" She spread her palms. "I don't know how I do it, sir."

"You don't?"

The crisped thing in the tank rotated a little, like a spit roast had been thrown in by accident. Tubes ran everywhere, some of them into where his face should be.

"Brittany, I don't care. Try. Do your best. Anything at all is better than letting him die without trying."

"There's something we haven't tried. What happened on the day I truly bonded with Jadd. When I kneeled for him and said my vows."

Words? He considered this. Maybe words had powers here, or perhaps it was something else. All he cared about was the result. "Do what you wish to. I'll watch over you both."

"Good." Jadd eyed the tank, saying nothing. The horror of what he saw seemed reflected in the small lines shifting about the man's eyes. "He's far gone. I love the man, but I don't know what trying this could do to her." Then he looked back at Brask. "If anything goes wrong, keep her safe, please."

She nestled into his side and whispered something Brask couldn't understand.

Meaning save her over him, if it came to that? He nodded. "I will."

*****

Kasper had not done the same thing again. He was like a creature with a bucket list to check off and once done, he moved on.

Chop off toe. *Check.*

Interrogate sternly. *Check.*

Deprive of food and water. *Check.*

At least they mostly left her alone in the room, as long as she didn't make too much noise. Willow sat on the edge of the bed and smoothed her palm over the sheet. Another day gone. They never changed the sheets and it was beginning to look grimy. No clothes still, but she was used to that. The men ignored her as if they were sexless.

She'd seen Ally yesterday while Kasper had talked. He seemed to like having both of them in the room at the same time when he was there. Though she was listless, her foot looked clean. It was bandaged even. Somehow they'd found a doctor, or maybe one of them was one? She had no clue.

Whatever they were waiting for, it was still coming. Nerve chewers. God. That scared her. Just the frickin' term did. The one or two men who'd seemed…human, had changed too. After they'd changed, she'd seen them with puncture marks on their hands and ankles like some gruesome stigmata. It had made her wonder if this was, after all, merely a cult.

Then something odd would happen. Kasper would just give her one of his lizard looks, and she'd go no, no way, these guys are not human anymore. A word Stom had once mentioned had popped into her head. Bak-lal. His people's enemies.

She'd used the word once to Kasper's face and he'd ordered her beaten. It wasn't conclusive. Hell, it meant zero really. That man was so fucking weird.

She followed the line of her chain leash to the new bolt on the wall. *Bastards.* They'd found out where she'd nearly pulled it off the headboard. Since Stom's collar was reinforced with metal and locked onto the leash, she'd tried the other end.

Fuck.

She flopped back and found the bit of paper under her pillow.

Whatever they were waiting for she had a feeling it was soon.

But last night something had happened.

On the lower edge of the piece of paper was a brown smudge. A char mark? She prayed it was that.

When all the lights went out, she took it out, put the pale thing before her eyes, and by moonlight she tried again. Staring. Concentrating. Thinking of Stom. Imagining what she could do if she could control fire, beautiful, beautiful fire.

Burn you little motherfucker.

Last night her arm mark had also burned. She'd woken and clutched at it. Real, or dream? Did it mean life or death? Or something else she couldn't conceive of?

Burn.

Like a sign of possibilities, an indefinite nibble played with her mind, calling her. When she tried to pin it down, the sensation vanished.

She concentrated again.

Burn.

*****

He awoke, floating. The world a muted pink, distorted. Specks drifted before his eyes. His mouth was wedged open. His skin felt wrong. All of him felt wrong. When he tried to move his arms and legs, to swim through this water, nothing had stirred despite the distinct sensation of his limbs moving.

His thoughts wandered for ages.

Until someone appeared miles away through the water. Their faces were bloated, wavering. Then he knew them, her, him. Jadd and Brittany. And he watched as she lowered herself and looked up at her man with her hands in his.

His heart awoke.

A glow expanded, jarred him, like an avalanche of crackling glass, and swept him away in the torrent.

Willow.

Flames. The bang and the whirlwind of fire. He'd tied her to the bed and, what, left her there. Why was he *here!*

Where was Willow?

He struggled then, making a monumental effort to erupt from what he now knew was a regen tank.

Then the true burning began. His skin was ripped into fragments of pure, piercing fire. He arched his body and he screamed. Slivers of torment began to cover his skin. He could see them, feel them assemble, piece by piece, in layer after layer, sucking on his agony, sticking to him, merging, lacing him with more fire.

Whatever had gone before, those memories of the explosion had been mostly lost, though he knew he'd come so close to dying that death had a skeletal hand on his throat and his balls. This slow knitting together, this exquisite torment of his body with needles, threads, and patches of fire – unforgettable agony.

He was a conflagration concerto in A major and someone was going to pay when he got out of here.

*****

The nerve chewers had arrived. She knew this because Kasper had ordered her brought into his torture room, as she'd decided to call it, to announce the arrival. She curled her hand around her charred piece of paper and went obediently with her handler, the leash dangling between them as he led the way. Down the hall, through the doorway.

Even if he had been taken over by some alien intelligence, she'd decided that some small part of him, perhaps the most creative part, was still Kasper. Unfortunately, it was the evil part.

He wasn't dispassionate after all, which was why he was telling her about his fresh pretty nerve chewers with Ally also in the room. The girl sat slumped in a chair.

Whatever their doctor had given her, it left her spaced out ninety percent of the time.

Ally's hair was so matted she ached to go to her and untangle it carefully. Then she would brush that long white-blonde hair that reached to her waist, and tie it in a bow, though Ally hated bows.

Kasper had said something else. She turned her head to listen.

"You will be second."

Which meant…

What he was about to say, she predicted even to the flash of menace in his dead eyes, and this was when she became totally certain some deeper portion of this creature remained the original evil man.

"And you will watch while we give it to her." He smiled. "While they begin their journey up her nerves to her brain, you will watch."

They pulled her to the wall and attached the leash to a bolt. They tied her hands then they began on Ally. When the girl was securely held down on her back by four men on the Persian rug, Kasper strolled to a table. He picked up a piece of equipment. It was only when he kneeled beside Ally to use it that she recognized it. A drill.

Sweat broke out all over her body.

The stigmata. The screams. This was what they did.

The whine lanced straight through her and her head filled with Ally's shrieks. Though she shut her eyes, squeezing them tight, she couldn't block those out.

The paper in her palm grew hot, hotter. The temperature climbed and climbed and though she became convinced her hand was alight she said nothing.

The screaming continued. The drill stopped and began again, vibrating into her gut.

She uncurled her hand, cleared the phlegm gathering in her throat, and forced open her eyes. Her throat shook with the hard beat of her heart.

Her hand seemed far away and the tears made it difficult to see, but she focused on the black fragments on her palm. There was nothing left but crispy shreds.

Shit.

She would burn through the leather they'd tied her with, break loose, and turn them all into dead men. But though she tried and tried, until sweat slicked her body and her head pounded, nothing had happened by the time they freed her. Her lunge toward Ally came to nothing.

"Let me see her, please. Let me see her. Please!" She dug her heels in but the man holding her leash dragged her toward the door.

Kasper inclined his head. "You can see her. There she is. Tomorrow, if she has survived, we will do this to you."

Willow didn't look. She didn't want to see more blood on Ally. She'd wanted to touch her, to hug her, to hide her in her arms and whisper that somehow she'd make things right, even if…even if she couldn't.

Those sounds she heard. She knew them. She didn't want to see her seizing. The sounds were Ally tapping her heels on the floor and her jaw clicking. She'd seen it in patients at the hospital.

Wrapping her hand around the leash only made her staggering progress across the floor a little slower.

Outside she heard doors slamming and the rumble of truck engines. Voices. The tramp of boots on the floor. Kasper nodded at the men walking into the room. More of the enemy.

They were lost. So terribly lost.

Her poor, poor girl.

Things of the nastiest kind had preoccupied her but now, between the dragging of her heels across the rug and the tromp of boots, the indefinable nibble returned and grew, and slammed into her with the subtlety of a man pushing her into a wall and kissing her.

Stom, she mouthed.

She could feel him. She put her hand to her breast, smiling in wonder, feeling the beat. *Thump*. A man who had somehow wormed his way into her soul, as well as her panties. A man who she suspected had his name tattooed on the underside of her heart.

She went to her knees and looked upwards, waiting. The creature holding the leash turned to stare at her.

Where are you?

Chapter 22

He opened his eyes, assessing where his body said she was. The pull was strong. So close. Stom leaned over the co-driver's shoulder and tapped the electronic map. "The next street over. About there."

The man spoke quietly. "Operations control? Can I have a visual on the possible house from data extrapolation?" The screen wavered and snapped to a top down view in shades of blue with what seemed to be people shown as red. They moved and there were so many.

Was she there? His heart said so.

"That's it," he said to Stom before turning back to the screen. "Operation control, I see forty-three enemy. The women's location?" He tapped the screen again. It zoomed into a view of one room. "There. Is this attack approved? We have a target! Go."

The driver accelerated.

Yes.

Stom said a quick and urgent prayer then tugged on the belt linking him to the ceiling of the van. The side door had hummed open minutes ago and he'd grabbed a handhold to stop himself falling out the door and onto the road that zipped past. Whatever the human speed limit was here, the driver was now exceeding it. Instant maiming if he fell.

Though maybe not. He eyed again his lower torso where the ceram suit ended at his waist. Brask hadn't let them crank him into a full suit, only

Jadd and a couple of others were trained for that. The powered, armored suit clung to you like it wanted to have sex with you and was capable of bouncing you around like an ape on stimulants. They were scared his new flesh wouldn't take the g forces on his upper torso.

He swallowed, swaying into the swerve, staring at the pinkness on his chest visible under his black shirt. Not much of him was the old him. Baby man, that was him. All pink and hairless. His Feya markings were mostly gone. His bond mate marking was so faint.

Who cared? All that mattered was finding Willow.

The Preyfinder coat whipped out behind him and flapped in Jadd's face.

"Control that thing," he yelled. "When we hit the ground, I'll watch your back, Stom. No hero stuff from you. I'll take point."

He growled. "You and Brittany might have saved me and I'll never forget that, but don't stop me reaching Willow."

The assessing nod from Jadd said, *sure, but I'll do my duty by you too*. He suspected that meant, he was number one and Willow was second. That would not go well. Maybe he should get there first. These suit legs could do some mean jumps.

Operations beeped on in his ear comm with a global message to the attack team. "Surveillance shows multiple new Bak-lal arriving. Now sixty plus. Don't move in until Accor's team gets there."

There were nine of them packed in this van, including the driver and co-driver. They'd all be fighting on this mission. With only human weapons and the armored coats the odds weren't great. Brask hadn't yet dared to approve off-world weaponry. If only Dassenze were back.

The co-driver spoke up. "The screen shows one of the women has multiple injuries. Her life signs are going crazy."

"Which one?" Stom croaked out. His voice wasn't so good. "Which one is injured?"

"Don't know, sir. The drone is going on body heat and audible data. We don't know which is her. Operations, advise when Accor is in range."

The van screeched around the corner, pulled to the side.

Mission control's reply sank into Stom's head and resonated. "Acknowledged."

There were times you just had to act.

He leaned down to check the map, unclicked the belt above, stepped out the door onto the road, and jumped. The engines in the legs detected his need for boost and kicked in with a complaining whine. The pale blue sky flew past. The house roofs became his landing points and he bounced from one to the other, leaving shattered tiles and dented roofing iron on the way.

Willow was worth it. He pulled out two grenades and linked his retinal display with that room as he went. He knew where the women were held; now all he had to do was neutralize everyone else.

On his way over the front yard, where a whole posse of Bak-lal was peering up at him with their blank-eyed expression, he tossed down the two grenades. One-story house. The roof was tiles and he landed above the room where they were.

Stom took another leap fifty feet upwards, spiraled to wrap the coat about his body, and came straight down on both boots. Tiles, timber and ceiling caved in. Something tore along the coat but spun off. The room was revealed. Plaster and timber fragments whizzed out like a flock of angry bees. Willow was to the left. Ally to the right. He hit on the floor and sank to one knee, the armored joints screaming as they compensated. His guns were already out and spitting bullets. Men fell as they reached for their weapons, spinning from the impact of the projectiles.

Blood sprayed. People shouted.

Got the one holding Willow and the four around Ally. A tall one, with some metal thing in his hand, sneered at him and roared, waving at others.

The room filled with sound and blood and whirling figures. He twisted, still shooting.

A horde of men piled toward him, reckless, disregarding the lethality of his presence. Shining blades glanced off the coat. The ones that came toward his face he batted away. Under the sheer weight of six or seven of them he fell, still fighting, one gun skidding away, the other under him. His wrist cracked and fractured.

Pain speared through him.

What a waste. He only just got that healed.

He was losing.

Desperately he threw out an arm to tell Willow to run. More Bak-lal poured in, mouths open, teeth showing, guns raised. What a mess. Brask was going to hate having to bury him again.

Worth a try. It was Ally dying, he'd seen her wounds, but it didn't matter. If he let her die without trying, Willow would been destroyed by grief.

The face of a Bak-lal obscured the ceiling as he scrambled atop the pile of men who were crushing Stom. One of his arms was trapped, but with the free one he warded off blows, then he kicked out with his legs. Two of the enemy flew out, smacked into the walls, and kept going, leaving body-sized holes. The top Bak-lal's pistol swung, coming in to aim at his head.

The rattle and crack of weapons told of the team arriving outside. A new hole or three appeared in the walls, blasting out chunks of plaster and timber. His ears hurt from the sound, his skin hurt, his muscles burned. The air misted with white.

He bared his teeth as the trigger was drawn back.

Like an avenging demoness, Willow leapt on top, naked, snarling, standing on the writhing heap. As she lashed out and clawed at the eyes of the one leveling his gun, the barrel swung and fired to the left. The Bak-lal grabbed her throat, held her still, her feet dangling, and shoved the gun at her side.

He couldn't move. He couldn't *move*.

*****

The gun was coming her way. Willow stared into death's eyes, her fingernails had left red scored grooves on his face but the man wasn't registering pain. Why couldn't she do more? She sobbed. They were both going to fucking *die*.

She'd been trying to set these bastards alight. Nothing.

His hand on her throat was choking her and she sucked in a wretched gasp of air, her vision smudging as her brain faltered.

The metal of the gun jabbed into her ribs. She was a half second away from having her guts blown across the room. *Why couldn't she?*

Burn.

Think small. Eyes? Oh. Yeah. Course.

His eyeballs burst into flame, a simmering orange.

Seemed even Bak-lal hated having their eyes on fire. He released her, dropped the gun, and toppled off the pile of men, screeching, with his hands scrabbling at his face.

The small success stunned her for one millisecond then she went ballistic on the pile.

Slap their faces and burn them. The growling ones that turned to get her were the first to go.

Burn, she hissed into their blank faces.

The only drawback: she had to touch them to do it. Dirty, disgusting work. Bad. And every one she hurt, they seemed *people* somehow, it made her shudder inside. *I'm weak.*

Horrifying, but it worked. She lost a few layers of her soul, but she didn't stop. She kept going, she burned them, and she freed him.

The room filled with writhing men clutching at their burning eyes. The Preyfinders picked them off. The battle rolled on. Bullets spat. Stom dragged himself to his feet and swept her off to the side, one blood-smeared arm dangling at his side. Then he enfolded her in his coat.

Ally.

There she was, where she'd last been, only with Kasper straddling her. The drill was in his hand, poised above, ready it seemed, to be driven into her skull.

No. Frantic she tried to leap toward her.

But Stom fought her. He held her tighter, wrapped the coat around her more.

"No, Willow, no. You can't. There're more bullets than oxygen out there. No."

He was gasping for breath and fresh blood welled from the side of his neck.

Watching Ally die was going to etch itself into her memories, but this time, because she knew it might be the last thing she could do for her, to honor her life, she watched. Despite wanting to reach out and drag her to safety and not being able to do a damn thing, she watched.

Ally's hand shot up, fingers splayed, and Kasper froze. What happened next was inexplicable. Impossible. She rewound what she'd seen.

Men were struggling, falling, and partly obscuring her view. There was a series of bangs as one huge Preyfinder leveled his weapon and emptied it into Kasper. He slumped to the floor, coughing out his last breath.

That part was good.

Except Ally was gone.

"Where is she? Stom? Ally's vanished! Where can she be?"

"Don't know." He slid down the wall, taking her with him and she pressed her hand on the neck wound, his blood welling through her fingers, her pulse hammering at her. If he died after this…

"Don't you die on me again, Stom, you bastard. Don't you dare!"

A whistle made her whip her head around, teeth bared, ready to turn into a crispy thing anyone who dared threaten her mate. A Preyfinder advanced on them.

"I'm Brask, Willow. I'm his friend." He ducked his head and peered at Stom. "You be good, man. We already spent a year's revenue on you. You owe us."

"Will he be okay?" She sniffed and looked from her man to Brask and back.

"Sure I will." Stom spat blood to one side. "Fine. I am. I'm definitely fine."

Behind Brask the fighting sounds had petered out to nothing.

"Yeah, he'll be okay. I have his read-outs. He's wired up and scanned. Neck wound's bleeding, that's all." Brask grinned. "We can rebuild him. Make him better than he was."

She scowled. "That's an ancient movie quote, isn't it?" Sick man. Aliens apparently equaled a bad sense of humor.

Relief washed in. She swayed on her knees, still perplexed. Where was Ally?

"You need to find my cousin, Brask. Please. She's gone. She was here."

"I know." He tapped his ear. "The drone above. The orbiting scan even. She disappeared from both. I have no idea where to. Here. Last image from Rimill. He's the one who shot your big bad guy. Kaper?"

"Kasper," she whispered. A video played out in the air in front of her. It looked taken from the side, perhaps down the sights of a gun. Ally, eyes wide open, hand outstretched, staring at Kasper, who didn't move. He was stuck in position, ready to kill her with that drill.

Then the gun must have fired because the image blurred a little. Kasper died, with holes appearing in his neck, side, head. And Ally…she was there, and then, she was not.

Something was left hanging in the air. The glimmer of metal? Tiny metal confetti rained down. When this Rimill moved in closer and, with his boot, tossed aside Kasper, she saw the confetti had settled on the floor in the shape of Ally's limbs.

"What's that?" she asked Brask.

"The residue on the floor? Not sure yet. Seems possibly infectious, even possibly alive. It's moving. My men have sampled it and we've fried the rest and bottled it too. I don't know what it is, except it's not a normal part of a human."

She lowered her pointing hand, and thought for a moment. Ally had seemed more awake than before. "Nerve chewers," she said quietly.

"What? What are they?" He leaned in. "Tell me."

"They're something your enemies are using to take over our heads. I think she's spat them out somehow. Rejected them. I think. I hope." Ally had kept their house safe for over ten years and she'd not suspected. What else could the girl do? Lots, she prayed. "And also...I don't know because this is a crazy idea, but then *all* of this is crazy." She heaved in a big breath. "I think she managed to escape somehow."

"What do you mean?"

"She's gone somewhere, and don't ask me where. Just, somewhere."

"We'll keep that in mind."

He didn't believe her. Maybe she was wrong but she didn't want to lose hope. Not now. A caress of her cheek made her turn her head into Stom's hand. She kissed his palm.

"You stay still, mister. Be good or else."

He chuckled and whispered. "Wait until I'm healthy, woman."

"I will. Soon, that better be. Soon." Willow snuggled into him.

The medics arrived to haul out Stom and patch him up and she went with them, hearing sirens in the distance and wondering how the Preyfinders were going to get out of this mess.

When they walked out, she saw the smoke pouring from a small fire in the house. There were holes in some of the adjacent houses. Bodies everywhere. Standing a few hundred yards back were people filming with phones. People would know now, wouldn't they? Half the damn city would know. Did it matter anymore? Seemed like the world was about to fall apart. Maybe these guys, for all their superior alien crap, needed some human help after all?

Whatever. She climbed into the open side door on the super duper shiny spaceship craft that settled on the lawn, sat down next to Stom with Brask opposite. A car loaded with men swerved into the driveway and men, obviously Bak-lal, spewed out, guns bristling.

"Lethal force approved," Brask muttered.

A pink ray blasted down from somewhere above, blatting the car into a flat, melted mess and sizzling every Bak-lal into a charred lump that smoked.

Her mouth dropped open. *Pink?*

"You in a mood?" Stom drawled.

"I'm tired. Besides, it needed doing, and I think we've already lost the 'pretend we're not here' option." Brask nodded, grimacing a little. "And it made me happy."

"There is that." He settled back into his padded seat and closed his eyes.

Worried, Willow observed him for a while. He was so pale, and different without his stripes. The medics had fixed the wound and pumped drugs into him. She sneaked her hand under his and nestled up to his side, happy when he tightened his hold on her for a moment.

"You're concerned about Ally?" he murmured, eyes still closed.

"Yes."

"You're close. Like you and I are. Ever think that if there was something wrong with her, you'd know?"

She thought that through. "Maybe. I'd like to think she's somewhere safe. Whatever she did it was considered impossible up to now. I think maybe she's tougher than I ever thought she could be."

"Then I think we should believe she's okay unless we find it's otherwise. Brask is going to mount a big search for her. So let's hang onto that hope. You, me. Okay?"

She smiled up at him. "Sure. Thank you."

"Mmm. I'm going to sleep now."

"Okay," she whispered. He needed to. He might be big and bad and one mean alien warrior but right now, he needed rest.

The engines hummed.

Down below someone waved to her, so she waved back at the poor humans as they took off. She had escaped that horror. How in the hell had she managed that? The trembling began but she strained and kept it to a minimum by remembering that she had Stom back. He was next to her, again. Hers, again. Warm, real, solid. Right now wasn't the time for breaking apart.

Gently, so as not to disturb him, she lay across his lap with her arm across his thighs, and shut her eyes. Now, all was quiet. This intimacy, she required it to survive as much as she did blood in her veins.

"Hey there," he whispered, fingering her ear and hair.

"Thank you." She hugged his legs.

"For what?"

For rescuing her. For coming when she needed him even though she'd stuffed up and almost gotten him killed. For being someone she could hold onto. By the time she'd gone through all that he was snoring but she said it anyway, smiling a little. "For being you."

One thought stayed with her all the way to the Preyfinder base: If only Ally were here.

Chapter 23

Willow sat beside Stom with her legs dangling over the edge. Water lapped at her toes. The glasslike half-dome pool with the up-lights was a few feet below but every now and then she felt as if she was in danger of falling straight out into space. Earth bobbed out there. The lower half of the globe was seemingly submerged in the blue pool, the rest floating in space.

Awestruck yet again, she bumped Stom with her shoulder. "This is so beautiful."

"Tenth time you've said that."

"So? It's true."

"Yes. I agree. It is."

She could see the small smile creep onto his mouth and ventured to ask, "You don't mind being stuck here with me? Having to be near Earth?"

The way he looked at her made her blush – studying her face for a few precious seconds before lowering his eyes to her breasts then even lower. They were both naked.

He raised a brow. "No."

The only answer to that was to roll her eyes, but she put her hand on his thigh. When he laced his fingers into hers, she angled her head and studied their hands. Next to their hands, his cock was rising.

"Whatever is that?" she asked in a horrified tone.

"Hmm. No idea, woman but it's all your fault."

She laughed. They'd had sex in the pool only twenty minutes before. She looked back at Earth. "Stom. When are we going back down? To the surface?"

"Soon. I asked Brask. They're letting me heal a bit more before reinstating me as a Preyfinder."

His stripes were slowly returning. The one curling under his nipple tempted her to follow it with her tongue. "Is there any news of Ally?"

"No, none as yet, but the Australian government is helping us now. If she's still on that continent, we'll find her eventually. Brask told me that Rimill has been keenly interested in finding her."

Cautious, she only said, "Oh?"

He stayed silent so she nudged him.

"Got a question for me, pretty girl?"

"Damn, you're trying to exasperate me!"

"No idea what that word means." He grinned.

They'd talked about how he and her had connected and also Jadd and Brittany. There seemed an innate attraction that had kicked in far too early for it to be the pet nano-chem. Something odd was happening and pairing up Earth women with specific alien men. Something that, perhaps, also brought out the women's powers.

"Do you think he's like us…and that it means she's still alive?" Now that would be the *best*.

Stom looked out into space a while. His feet stirred the pool water. "Yes. I do, but don't get your hopes up too much."

Then she wouldn't tell him how the news had her heart leaping about like a baby deer in spring. "I won't."

"Liar."

She chuckled and leaned in, thinking about nipping his nipple. His hand whipped out from her grasp and grabbed her hair.

"*Do not* unless you want a spanking."

"That's supposed to stop me?"

The growl in his chest made her shiver.

But he let her go and climbed to his feet. Then he held out his hand and drew her up. "Stand there beside the bed."

Despite her pointed look of puzzlement, he left the room.

The dim lighting and the proliferation of tropical plants on the walls and in pots on the floor, gave this whole room the atmosphere of a lush jungle. Deliberate perhaps. This *World* room on the orbital platform was meant as a special treat to the men and women resting from their duties on Earth.

She'd been wondering all day if Stom was up to something and he returned carrying a tray that he set down on the quilt of the huge square bed. She followed his every move. The man had a body that dominated wherever he walked. The flow of his muscles made her want to worship all of him, to tell him to walk around some more so she could see his ass.

He had some plan. She frowned.

On the tray was a paint brush with a tube feeding into the back of it as well as various pots of sealed color.

"You're to stay still, even if I tickle you. I'm going to take off your collar but I'll put it back on afterward. You'll never not be my pet, gorgeous one, but this is different."

That had her going *hmm* and sucking in her lower lip "Okay. What are you going to do?"

"Shh." He unlocked her collar and put it aside then picked up the brush and plugged it into a pot of red. "My color goes on first."

The first brush stroke began on her neck. She watched as he applied fine whorls and lines and dots of paint to her body. Stom had never seemed an artist. He built up the design, color by color. The tip of the brush did tickle her when he swirled around her red nipples and across her belly but she bit her lip and stayed still and silent. The lights hidden among the plants on the walls washed over her and made her gleam where the paint stayed wet.

He paused a moment and his lips curved upward at one corner. "This will make you mine."

She'd thought she already was. Her thoughts must have showed.

"I'll explain when I'm done." The understanding crinkle around his eyes endeared him to her yet again. Then he continued painting her, adding gold and a luminescent pink.

He was quiet and gentle, and dedicated to this, so she turned when he asked and smiled at the serious way a little crease appeared on his brow while he worked. When the brush strayed onto her sex and stayed there while he did minute strokes, before moving on to embellish her inner thighs, her breaths deepened.

And when he dabbed her clit with a swirl of orange, she squeaked. "Bad man."

"I am, aren't I? I want to lick you there but it would spoil the design."

Damn. But she stood straighter. He continued around to her ass then down her legs.

When at last he straightened and stood back, admiring her, she merely smiled and waited.

"Turn." He circled his finger and she obediently turned.

"Am I done?"

"Yes. You, are so, *so* beautiful."

Aww. When he said that she wanted to hug him. "What does it mean?"

"It's the Feya way when two bond mates take the final step. It's our way of affirming our love for each other. Now you." He handed her the brush.

Love? She almost squealed at that.

"But…" She eyed his naked body, thinking of how she might violate some ancient painting tradition if she slipped. Was there a template? A drawing? "I don't know how to do it."

"There is no proper way. Every couple is different. Paint me as you wish to."

"Oh. Is it permanent?"

"No, it will wash off over a few days."

She took the brush and thought. Then she began with his chest and, like he had, she drew many designs. When she looked askance of him after the first daisy below his nipple, he smiled. With more confidence she continued, each addition built on the idea that in doing this she was claiming him, as he had claimed her.

When she too stepped away, there was almost no surface over which she had not run her brush. Stom was warrior red and orange with his muscles delineated and emphasized. A dark blue made small pretty shading in places. She adored his masculine beauty. His strength, his confidence, his willingness to devote himself utterly when it was needed, this too was a true part of him she valued dearly. The Feya stripes she had reinforced and darkened with more black and gray, because they meant Stom to her. There was only one place left she hadn't done, so she knelt before him and eyed his cock, quirked her brow. "May I?"

"Yes." He touched her hair, moving away a few strands that had fallen over her nose. "If you wish. The paint is safe."

"Ahh." Emboldened, she carefully painted a blue and red helix design on his cock, pleased to see how it rose more and more erect as she worked. By the time she was done, Stom had a supreme erection she figured might rival the Eiffel Tower, and she had a peculiar feeling of lightness, as if she might float off the floor. She stood and put aside the brush, then walked around him once, admiring her alien lover.

"Come." Stom beckoned to her and, without him voicing it, she knew what she should do. She let him pick her up and, when she felt him in the right place, she sank down on him, watching his face, marveling.

When at last, he was deep inside, Stom sighed.

They kissed as if each were some delicate thing that might be crushed, and ascended toward orgasm slowly, panting, but with minimal noises. She rode him up and down, appreciating every inch of him, absorbed in the sensations, biting his neck then moaning when he in turn bit hers. When she came, gasping softly, he did also. It was simple and quiet and a reaffirming of who they were to each other. The thump at her temples lessened and she realized her breathing had synchronized with his.

As if anointing her, he kissed her mouth, her nose, her forehead, her neck, then he waited, his eyes on hers. The clarity of the blue of his irises, and that he was still inside her, holding her to him, struck her. This was so right.

"We are one," he murmured. With the hand at her nape, he rearranged her hair, stroking her. She could tell he had more he wished to say and so she waited without speaking. His sigh seemed to travel all the way to her toes. "Willow. I love you."

If she screamed he might drop her, so she grinned instead. "Yay."

He'd said the words. She'd known he would, one day.

"And I love you."

"Mmm. I thought so." He mouthed her neck then rested his forehead on hers and spoke with his lips an inch away from hers, their breaths mingling.

"Did you know that your fingers were on fire when you came?"

"No!" Alarmed, she checked, expecting to see burns on his skin. He was perfect. Unharmed.

"I saw it, but couldn't feel it."

What did she say to that? "Sorry?"

"Forgiven, my love. Next time we might try the pool again. Just in case."

She grinned and hugged his neck. "Crazy man."

"Yes. I think I must be. But if you ever set my cock on fire, I will spank you, very, very hard."

Chapter 24

Rimmil strapped on the small arsenal they'd allowed him. The squad was readying for yet another aerial and ground search of the coastline, north of Brisbane. That Brask put some weighting on his, Rimmil's, guess that the missing woman had gone in that direction seemed strange. He hadn't been told why. He knew Jadd's and Stom's histories. It was ridiculous to assume that minor sexual intrigue might mean anything.

He'd not even touched her. All he'd done was shoot the Bak-lal about to kill her. That and filmed her disappearance.

He shut his eyes. There she was, flawed, yet in an ethereal and ominous way, beautiful. White hair spread about her in a halo of brightness that drew him. And then her eyes, her white eyes. Why had no one else remarked on her white eyes?

Every tendon in her hand was taut as she somehow froze that man. The drill above. Blood dripping from her hand and down her wrist.

Then. Gone.

He slipped his Berskald rifle into the sling. They could use their weapons now, within limits. No disturbing the natives, of course. Unless they were enemy.

Things were changing.

Beep. Operations control. *Global message*, said the fine print on his retina.

"News: an astronaut launched into space by the Chinese government was a Bak-lal. From orbit, she sent a focused message to the enemy. Expect the unexpected from now on. This planet will now be on the Bak-lal agenda for invasion."

*****

Ally took a breath and smiled. The grass stems around her head swayed in the breeze. The tiny purple blossoms dotted on the stem were as pretty as a whole vase of cut flowers. She loved the small things of nature. This farm was a lonely one, lost on a back road miles from the main highway, with only Mrs. Stewart and her. On the day she'd arrived in the kitchen garden, the poor woman had looked astonished.

Her toe ached like crazy now and then but she'd grown used to that and Mrs. Stewart thought the stitches looked fine. She couldn't remember the suturing. Someone had cut off her toe then stitched her up and kept it clean, maybe given her antibiotics.

The disharmony in that made what had been done seem more evil than just chopping it off.

She shivered. Those days were hazy memories. Except the last minutes, last harrowing seconds, when she'd done something to that half man-thing who'd wanted to kill her.

It was calm here though. Beautiful. She shivered again but from a stunned sort of wonder.

Outside. She was *outside*. Sun on her face. Wind. Living plants, grass, trees, birds. Birds were the best. She'd often watched them from her window. Those few times she'd managed to climb the reservoir with Willow and lain down on her back to stare up at the evening or morning sky, there'd been birds passing overhead. Birds said freedom.

If she didn't go inside soon, Mrs. Stewart would chastise her for getting sunburned. Ally grinned. Sunburned. How amazing was that? Maybe her skin would even peel like Willow's had.

Willow was the one thing she missed, but she'd see her again soon. Soon as she worked out what to do.

She and Mrs. Stewart had read the news announcements together and decided it was for the best if she stayed anonymous for now. Until she got more practice. People wanted her to help them. That idea, she liked in theory. Reality though... *Hmm.*

The sun was over there beyond her left shoulder and a cow was munching grass to the right. The third Bak-lal in a week was four hundred yards over farther. Random. But dangerous.

She'd stay silent. He'd wander off or Mrs. Stewart would kill him. There was that too. The woman was good with a shotgun.

The scritching in her head intensified. *Crap.* More pain killers needed, especially with her foot now throbbing also. That one nerve chewer left was going to have to go once she figured out how to shift again. In a way, she could *see* it, could make it stay put, but one day it might get loose. Disaster, if that happened. If she wanted to deal with those who had hurt her and Willow, she needed to get rid of it.

The day of the battle flocked into her head, spinning, making her nauseous again. Black coats, red blood, screaming, people dying. The noise of thoughts. Death. *God.* Her head nearly exploded again. She'd be no use to anyone insane.

Epilogue

He's here.

Talia surveyed the floor under the heels of her tan boots, trying to seem nonchalant and innocent. Her butt was hurting. She'd been sitting here too long, but the noises said they were approaching – the *thwumm* sound of their unshielded engines. Below, the lifts had started up and there were stealthy footsteps on the stairs coming down from the rooftop. Their craft must be hovering somewhere in the sky outside this skyscraper. She was on the nineteenth floor, so it could only be that.

It had taken her weeks to find some Bak-lal she could use. But now, he was coming too.

No more avoiding her. If she couldn't get to him, he would come to her. Her text had mentioned his name. She bet that had grabbed his attention.

The news headlines were screaming things like *Aliens are real*, *The flying saucer has landed*, and, *Should we shake hands with aliens?* It hadn't taken long for her memory to jigsaw itself back together.

She remembered the killing, the bodies, blood. Remembered being fast and deadly and the gleam in the man's eye as he watched her. He'd said her sister's name.

There'd been nothing in the news about missing women, but she remembered him taunting her. Brittany was alive.

Her memory wasn't perfect, but she knew he was an alien. Brask. One of the Preyfinders, as they called themselves in the news. Finders of the evil Bak-lal aliens, or so they said – she wasn't taking anything at face value.

The more she thought about him, the more dangerous he seemed. The more he bothered her. Gut instincts? Subconscious impressions? Whatever, she knew he wasn't just a fighter. He'd been as intrigued by her as she was with him. She'd imagined him touching her, her touching him, and she'd thought over and over about that so much that it frustrated her. Then she'd fantasized about putting a sword through him.

Being near him did something to her and if she found out it wasn't natural, she was going to be extremely unhappy.

But…she flexed her hand, watching the tendons shift. Would he come?

The door at her back banged as the man inside butted into it again. She'd done her best but like this, alone, seemed she wasn't as fast as she recalled.

He, Brask, must be the key. Her analytical brain had tweaked her, whistled, and said, *Hey, stupid, when he was around you were like the fucking wind.*

"Bugger the wind," she muttered.

Men slinked from the stairway, guns out. The lift doors slid open and two more erupted from that then ran along the corridor toward her, covering each other. Brask exited behind them, slow and deliberate.

Electricity. The plucking of a thousand violins. And her heart sped up like she'd been racing a jet plane down a runway. Her ovaries waved maracas, just a little.

Fuck. She did not need this shit. "Not natural" fairly screamed its way into her head and bounced about waving a placard. *And* she needed a change of panties.

He was so hot the air should be steaming.

She yawned to cover up her sigh and struggled to her feet, her back sliding up the wall. So they could see she wasn't armed, she kept her hands out, and stepped away from the door.

"In there." She jerked her head at the door and went sideways. "Be careful. I only wounded him."

In a couple of seconds, they'd scanned the door with some device, booted it open, and scampered in to restrain the poor guy. One of them, the last through, flinched as he stepped over the threshold, and looked back at her.

She shrugged. "He tried to kill me but the news report said you wanted one alive. I figured you'd get here quickly."

Cutting off his hand had been her last resort. The bugger was fast and he hadn't bled as much as a normal human should either. The small sounds as they restrained him became background noise. Brask had arrived.

In one hand was a katana. A real one. Edo period possibly. Worth oodles.

It seemed wise to keep some distance, so she backed off. Already, her body felt more alive. Like she could stick to the ceiling and run along. Ninja moves, and she wasn't blinking much either. Her hand itched for the sword.

He holstered his pistol under his coat and she caught a glimpse of a second holster.

"Hello, Talia." Brask smiled a smile that didn't quite reach his eyes. "You called?"

"I did," she drawled. "I remembered you. Where is my sister?"

The hiss through his teeth sounded exasperated, yet he looked her up and down in a leisurely way – the way of a man assessing a pretty body.

"Up here." She indicated her face.

That got her a proper smile. "It's lucky I like what I see."

"Why?" Arrogant smarmy bastard.

"This is for you." He held out the sword, his fist around the scabbard. "I noticed you liked them – Japanese swords."

"Again, why? I just want my sister back. If you, whatever you are, if you have hurt her…"

"No. We haven't. I'm giving you the sword as a gift."

"A gift?" She adjusted her stance, certain that he expected more than a thank you in return.

The Preyfinders had taken the man further inside, toward the apartment window, and from the sounds of it, were evacuating him via that onto the flying craft.

"Thank you for finding the Bak-lal. There are very few being detected and we needed a live one."

"You're welcome." She didn't budge and waited for him to lower the sword. Didn't tell him that she could detect a Bak-lal when she saw one, feel the nasty vibes, identify the difference in how they moved. It made her wonder about why she felt him when he was near too. "My sister?"

"You know," he added, as if he'd read her mind, "I could tell you were here, in this building, before I saw you. I could sense you."

The subtle twitch of his lips said it meant more to him than she guessed, and he wanted her to ask him for the reason.

"So? I can tell when you're near." Though she was dying to understand, it was never going to be said. She was not going to feed his arrogance.

"You want to know about your sister? You'll find out, after I kiss you, once you're mine." As he'd spoken, his hand had darted toward her wrist.

She let him try, but twisted aside at the last second and skipped backward. The reverberation of that near touch hummed through her in a small earthquake of arousal. *Damn.*

Kissing him. What an idea. She couldn't stop herself staring. Tall but with a solid physique. He looked constructed just so a woman could trace her finger along his muscles. Gold glints at the tips of his short blond hair, mean looking, with a big M. Those weird blue cheek tattoos. Just her type.

Sure, she could go with kissing him. If she didn't have a brain.

Her mouth was open. She snapped it shut.

She could resist. He entranced her, but she could resist.

"Whatever the fuck you are doing to me, mister, it isn't going to work. Tell me or I go to the news with my suspicions about what you're doing to women. You want us to help you against these Bak-lal? I promise you, if people hear about women being kidnapped by aliens, they aren't going to be friendly."

He'd never kiss her because whenever he came close, she went all ninja-fied. She breathed in deep and regular, watching the hallway sparkle with information. Yes. She *could* run on the ceiling for, *ohhh*, about a half second, bounce off it anyway, and even that was awesomeness multiplied. If she'd eaten her oatmeal this morning she'd maybe do it longer.

She swore his nostrils had flared at her statement, like a bull about to charge.

"Oh, it'll work, Talia. Once I get reinforcements."

"Reinforcements?" She chuckled, ignoring the wave of goose bumps that had swept her at his threat. "To kiss me?"

Impasse. Her threat was shaky. She had no evidence and, if she made these guys angry, who knew what they'd do to her sister? *Bugger.*

She shoved back her hair from her face, scowled.

"Let me raise the stakes. Give me back my sister and I'll find you more of them." She indicated the door and threw her card on the table. "I can see Bak-lal. I can find more for you."

"Can you now?" From the tone, that intrigued him. "But you're going to tell me anyway, because we're going to be bond mates."

She cocked her head. "Say that again. What the hell are bond mates? No wait, don't answer. It's bad. I can tell. Let's stick to being polite to each other and you keep your dirty fantasies to yourself."

His reply was quiet yet assured. "You cannot avoid me forever. You see, Talia, there's a god interested in you, and nothing moves faster than him. Do you dare deny a god his desires? Do so and I guarantee *polite* is the very last word in your language that could be used to describe what will happen to you."

He was serious. This time the goose bumps went all the way to her nipples, which jutted out into her shirt and ached. A god? He must be joking?

The End

To join my mailing list and receive notice of future releases:

http://www.carisilverwood.net/about-me.html

Books by Cari Silverwood
http://www.carisilverwood.net/books.html

Connect with Cari Silverwood on Facebook
http://www.facebook.com/cari.silverwood

Cari Silverwood on Goodreads
http://www.goodreads.com/author/show/4912047.Cari_Silverwood

Also by Cari Silverwood

Preyfinders Series
Precious Sacrifice
(Published in the anthology, Kept. Soon to be released as a solo book)
Intimidator

Pierced Hearts Series
(Dark erotic fiction)
Take me, Break me
Bind and Keep me
Make me Yours Evermore

The Badass Brats Series
The Dom with a Safeword
The Dom on the Naughty List
The Dom with the Perfect Brats
The Dom with the Clever Tongue

Cataclysm Blues Series
Cataclysm Blues
(A free erotic scifi novella. Currently being turned into a trilogy)

The Steamwork Chronicles Series
Iron Dominance
Lust Plague
Steel Dominance

Others
31 Flavors of Kink
Three Days of Dominance
Rough Surrender
(Being re-released by Momentum, an eBook branch of Pan Macmillan)

Manufactured by Amazon.ca
Bolton, ON

26588205R00114